PART II

C. K. Conners

The Ramblings of a Small-Town What's-His-Name, Part II

First Edition - Paperback
Route 27 Publishing®

Book design by C. K. Conners

ISBN: 978-1-949045-02-4

Contents

CRITICS ARE RAVING!

"This is but a taste of what's to come—a second taste, rather. And, seeing as the first sampling was akin to Brussels sprouts dipped in apple cider vinegar toothpaste, I must acquiesce that, in selecting the sequel, I am but a shadow of my former, sophisticated self. Indeed, I am a broken man."

Roland Downe-D'River / *Proofreader, Proper Pontification Periodical*

"I judged a book by its cover, and in so doing have proved wrong the old adage. I judged this book would look great in a trash compactor. And I was right."

Arthur N. E. Cookies / *Blogger, I'm Fine: Surviving My Gluten-Free Marriage*

"While this is probably the first time in my life I have seen something through to completion, I fear this accomplishment comes at a terrible cost."

Kent Hackett / *Anticipated Author of the Yet Unfinished Book,* [Insert Title Here]

"I've made an appointment to have my brain checked."

Anna May Tedd / *Contributing Writer,* Sedentary Living Weekly *and Author,* Stoicism: Nature's Aging and Wrinkle Defense

---

"Boy, was I in for a surprise! Change can be scary—but how rewarding! I supped every morsel of this new adventure with rapturous delight! Each bite was filling; yet, I kept craving more! Another 4.5 star experience!"

Brian

[Full disclosure: So, yeah, this Brian guy keeps dropping in our review receptacle his praise for the seriously stupendous Italian eatery down the street. Still, one has to ask the question: With such glowing reviews, what's that 0.5 of a star Brian has now twice withheld, forbidding a perfect 5?]

"My doctor prescribed medication to get me through stressful, vexing situations. Conners has forced more than a dozen refills and three dosage hikes."

Sybil Dee Skord / *Host of the Thrice-Canceled Debate Show,* As If!

Introduction

THINGS are changing, my dear reader. Indeed, things *have* changed. In just a toddler's bound over a year, the very foundations of our operations here at Route 27 Publishing®, as well as those of the lonely party comprising this company, have been shaken by a most astounding tremor. And how these pages are filled with the echoes—the very music!—of its reformative undulations!

I may be getting ahead of myself.

Let's try this again.

WELCOME, dearest reader, to *The Ramblings of a Small-Town What's-His-Name, Part II*! I am, as always I have been and will be, your faithful narrator. If you survived the journey through Ramblings One and have returned to the Connerian table for a second helping, let me say, on behalf of all of us here at Route 27 Publishing®, we admire your tenacity and can fully relate to your reckless abandon. Attending with openness to the thoughts and ideas of others is a risky business these days—seems you've got some of the sterner stuff in you.

In case you've forgotten or blocked out the memory of our time together in the first installment of this series, or you are a curious grazer of literary sustenance, inspecting the first couple of pages for signs of nourishment to quell your literary cravings, I suppose it would behoove me to give myself a quick (re) introduction—just a quick one.

As stated, I am the narrator: a humble employee of one C. K. Conners, hired as a sort of translator of the mind to bring about upon the page in coherent fashion the wild designs spinning about the Author's head like beams from laser pens, clasped in the clammy hands of a school bus full of five-year-olds.

That was a bit long-winded and, perhaps, not the clearest of examples. Let's try on this one for size: If he (Conners) is the architect, I am the builder; if his work is the recipe, mine is the sizzling dish—though, it must be stated that the T-squares, hard hats, aprons, and chef's caps are not tools and attire exclusive always to just one of us. It's a harmonious partnership, his and mine, with ideas, pens, and fists all landing perfectly upon their marks in a creative process second to none: one of ink and blood, spilling plenty of both.

Having said all of that, however, allow me to toss into the works a jarring contradiction. While we do occupy a tandem writing desk for many of Conners' major works, we both like to fly solo every now and then; and that's what makes this series so unique. Here, in the world of Ramblings, Conners presents stories composed without my assistance, and I set them up in the prologues preceding them, providing inspirational history (that is, a history of the *eureka* moments that propelled his writing, rather than histories that bolster or motivate the spirit), along with some enriching context, and almost always tossing into the mix a sarcastic quip or two. These I write without his direct guidance or supervision. Mind you, this is not to say he doesn't *want* to see or does not explicitly instruct me to present my work for review before publication; rather, he first writes his pieces; then, I write mine; and, at long last, once the final stroke of my pen has fallen, finished copies somehow find themselves being pumped out of the printing press. A curious phenomenon. But, I mean, it's too late at that point for any review, right?

So, that's me: your faithful narrator, here once again to offer guidance and diversion, and presently burning the midnight oil in an effort to wrap up my work before the Author returns to the office to see just what I've been saying about him.

With that out of the way, I think we're just about ready to begin.

As in Ramblings One, there lie in the offing seven stories, along with seven prefatory pieces composed by yours truly. As for these so-titled Prologues, take them as you wish: before or after reading, in between sets of biceps blasting at the gym, with a spot of coffee and a crumbly crumpet, in a hole with a mole and a guy named Beau with a bandage wrapped around his hammer toe—however it suits you best. Some readers like to step blindly into the new world that is an unread tale; others prefer a sampling of its juices to whet the palate before sinking the literary dentures through the outer skin.

Really, the *modus operandi* of this series hasn't changed much—or, has it?

And, so, we return to my opening statement:

Things are changing, my dear reader; yes, indeed, things have changed.

O, that the point would hasten to his fingertips! Or that those tedious, key-tapping appendages would be struck lame, or with phalangeal muteness! Hast thou not enough trees already sacrificed upon the alter of wasting my time?

The gang's all here! Glad to have your sharp and eloquent tongue expectorating all over these pages, my dearest of readers. Feels like old times, now—doesn't it?

"Old times," sayest thou? Quite right, indeed, thou art—if in but one *sense of the phrase; for mine onion doth like the pungent vegetable 'neath*

the merciless sun sprout an abundant proclamation of the scourge of age! For these fading follicles have I thee to blame—and I do, most perfervidly!

And, there you have it, dear reader: my point.

You may discover, as you read, that change is a sort of motif of this book's entire presentation. Your agreeing with me, dear reader, is but the first example to rear its head; but, oh, how many more await you in the pages to come!

My employer is a very different man—insufferable still, yes; but different; and I think it's affecting me. It's affecting everything, actually: the process, the content, the drive, the focus, the vibe, the aura, the schedule, the waking, the sleeping, the dancing and prancing and even romancing…need I continue?

Just compare Ramblings One to Ramblings Two (beyond the shift from the number One to its successor). See how the cover and artwork has changed. Pay attention to how the illustrations herein bear a different style. And ask yourself, "Why?"

Consider the seven stories in the offing, as I hope you will. Conners is the same writer, indeed, as far as compositional ability and proclivity goes; but what of the man? Can you identify him? And what is version 2.0 when likened to the first? Even consider that, unlike the premier Ramblings publication, only six compiled herein follow the pattern established in the former—that goes for the prologues, too.

How much more there will be for you to find!

Indeed, I shan't give it all away just now. What fun would there be in that? Instead, let these lips, interpreted through these fingers, cease to wag (at least, until the next page); and let this narrator sweep aside the starting gate that is this Introduction, releasing you into the world of Ramblings, Part Two.

And, we're off!

Prologue: Dear Departing One

HOW better to hook the fish than with a bite-sized morsel? Indeed, one might nab a voracious shark by dangling an entire carcass before its peeled and greedy eyes; but not every reader is a ravenous *liter-avore*: a manic consumer of books with an insatiable appetite for characters, settings, plots, and the delectable words that burst the latter named into gushing explosions of literary flavor. Nay! Most readers have but time enough for that which comes in the form of phonetically-composed and grammar-deprived digital messages—and even *that* is too much for some!

Perhaps this is why you have come: short stories are quicker, easier, require less of a commitment, and get to the meat and cheese without having to bother with an obstructive layer of bread. You might even think, given publication history to date, that Conners' personality and manner reflects this style of literary brevity. You may very well assume he's a man of few words.

Should, indeed, you find yourself thinking this way, I advise you to quit this rebellious life of yours, and pick up the Ramblings series in chronological order; for such thinking is clear evidence that you've not read Ramblings One—at least, not all the way through to the end. And, if that is the case, you most certainly missed the second-to-last page, whereupon I composed a closing note.

If ever your stars crossed so clumsily and violently as to

upend one another onto the backside as they passed, rendering your path one with Conners', you would undoubtedly discover a man from whose face few words fall, but *of* whose face you'll certainly discover—simply fountaining from within you—a bounty of words to relate, provided your thesaurus has a broad web stemming from the adjective "alarming."

It makes one wonder, therefore, how it could be possible that his is seen by those closest to him as a most mobile mouth, one not viewed as a mere medium through which ideas, expression, and communication are conveyed, but rather as a black hole of sorts, one that dominates conversations, overpowers the senses, and crushes the will to endure. Those who by blood are bound to his very being were foredoomed at his conception to have their lives filled with all the tales he so urgently must tell. You, dear reader, on the other hand, have a choice; and, being that you're here, it seems you are making it. Whether you do so wisely remains yet to be seen.

One might chalk up this character trait of sorts to his hermitic lifestyle—such living is like a dam set against an unusually powerful flow of conversation, allowing none of the mounting pressure to be released until some poor, helpless passerby swings a tinker's hammer into the walls of that dam by way of a neighborly smile. By the time the senses recover, the poor soul is informed by a concerned loved one or emergency first responder that they have only narrowly survived a freak onslaught and avalanche of buoyant conversation, bellowed forth as a towering tidal wave, crashing true and without end into its mark, as would a barrage of missiles locked onto a most desired moving target.

In truth, a stranger need worry little. Conners understands

well that within the unknown surely lurks one whose tongue hurls words at a rate of fire far more daunting than his own, with possibly a greater magazine capacity to boot; and one, also, whose dam of isolation rises far higher, runs far deeper, and has become far more fragile than his; thus, he is cautious and calculated about those he approaches at random—a.k.a. no one. Still, those who are foolish enough to desire acquaintance will undoubtedly feel the fury of bottled loquacity, sooner or later.

Why, though, am I telling you this?

I won't try to discourage you from following my employer's work, lest I find myself out of a job; nor will I try to deter you from continuing with this book (Not like I'd have to do so—do you recall the Reader's Agreement on the copyright page, dear reader? If not, I advise you to review your "obligation"). No, what I'm endeavoring to do, rather, is prepare you for what is to come. Honestly, you have seen nothing yet.

And, so, I ask again: How better to hook the fish than with a bite-sized morsel?

If you answered, "Toss the hook and grab a net," I'd say, "You're cheating, but you might actually be on to something."

Our first story in this collection of seven was inspired and composed in the early daytime hours (a mere thirty minutes into the morning, to be exact), when the Author, amid watching a rerun of an old favorite TV show, became fascinated with a very serious reality.

A show about a pale-mustached physician, who solves murder mysteries in what must be the most perilous corner of California, this particular episode was rare in its plot, as it did not actually contain a murder. Rather, it centered around a friend of the bushy-lipped doctor, staring down a most terrifying road, from which they were powerless to depart.

As the episode closed, a final conversation was had between these two characters; and so powerful was this exchange that the Author whipped out his pen and began to scrawl. Though he had little idea where his story would go, he set out with the intent to explore this particular suffering, to capture its weight, search its every angle, and plumb its daunting depths.

One more thing before we begin: In *Dear Departing One*, you will find a scene crafted around an experience had by the Author during his college years. Though neither filled with high-octane moments or white whales, what the Author beheld this day has remained with him as a vivid memory, one which played before his eyes as his pen did scrawl.

It was a very simple scene: a person walking up and down a lonely sidewalk, every time for the first time.

Let's get started!

DEPARTING
ONE

Dear Departing One

A curious thing. A curious thing indeed.

TODAY I stumbled upon a house. Abandoned it was, *is*—must have been, must truly be—for in it I found no inhabitants. Though—a curious thing, thought I—*think* I—whoever had occupied this lovely dwelling had not left it long before I had arrived. In fact, I would wager they had vacated the premises just days before I'd found myself within its clean, well-decorated walls. And they have left everything, whoever they were: photographs, furniture; there is even food in the refrigerator, which is still running (though, not swiftly enough that I could not catch it—oh, well; I make myself laugh...whatever).

But, yes, how curious, thought I—*think* I—to find myself here, in a house that was a home just a short while ago, but is so no longer. And how handsome a home: bright walls, clean, as I have said; and tall, very tall; numerous rooms, all fresh and well-furnished with what I assume are rather expensive pieces (appraisals of such items are not exactly my forte; I'm a simple man); photographs of lovely people: a pair of strapping young boys; three gorgeous girls: an elder, quite elegant and exceptionally lovely; a scrappy-looking younger, with practical hair and dirty jeans, along with a most mischievous grin that certainly suggests *this* one, and her tattered attire, have, perhaps, a rather adventurous (and hopefully legal) story to tell; and an infant, dressed in the same outfit in which the woman holding her—an astonishingly handsome woman—must have dressed her doll when she was just a girl.

This woman, the one holding the babe: she is indeed of a rare variety of beauty! I dare say these eyes have never beheld such a vision. And whoever lived within these walls must have agreed, for her face appears frequently and in various stages of age. Here, in this photograph, holding the child, she is no older than forty—can't be. Here is another photograph—she is older; though, Age has failed to steal away even a shred of her beauty; I dare say she has so defied the scourge of Time in discovering a maturity like a flower that buds in springtime and knows never a dry day or the coming of autumn; only deeper, more intricate weavings of beauty does she wear upon her petals, and from her heart issues forth an aroma at which even angels stop to marvel.

On the mantle—here she is again: a fading photograph, tinted yellow, old; though, the one preserved within is full of youth. And here, resting upon this table, I see that she has repelled Age once again; the struggle, however, has begun to dye her hair with streaks of silver; the hue of a precious metal framing neatly some lucky fellow's most precious partner. Oh, what would it be to know her heart as one's own?

Her fair face, its curves and lines—they are oddly familiar. Why do I get the feeling I have seen this shape before? I suppose, since we as humans can become so captivated by beauty, beholding a vision, a variety of elegant loveliness so priceless and rare, one is bound to believe it is familiar; for who—even by way of self-deception—wouldn't want to know that such heavenliness is to their very being close and friendly? How curious this aching to understand, this pull to recall a name unknown: a sound never heard, a memory never made; a piece to a missing puzzle; something I have not; something I have never possessed.

A most handsome family, indeed.

A most handsome home.

And curious.

How curious.

Why so familiar, this woman? Indeed, in her company are, to these eyes, complete strangers, save for the elder girl, who appears as a youthful copy of she who is to me so oddly known. I look upon her, this matriarch, and I can faintly hear a voice—what I assume is *her* voice. She calls a name I do not know. She calls it gently, but it hangs heavily with silent anguish. Her voice is that of one missing someone nearby, someone in earshot. A mounding hopelessness fills the gentle sound of her call, her plea.

To whom is she calling?

I know not the name.

I know not her.

But I know I've seen her—recently.

Who is she?

I have checked every room, including the ones upstairs: the one with the bunk bed, the single window with the cracked sill, and blue walls, upon which giant photographs are plastered, photos of athletes and militant spacemen (that's my best guess, anyway); the one with the two windows, both circular in shape, and purple walls, whereby a single bed is nuzzled peacefully between the regal hue and an antique nightstand, upon which sits a phone and beneath which rests a backpack, its hefty contents, along with stacks of paper, strewn about the bed—all of this sitting opposite a bed with disturbed sheets, at the foot of which are filthy sneakers that point toward the rival wall, where stands a desk, upon which rises a fortress of glass housing a lizard; here, also, are scattered some dirty, junior geological matter and equipment. And then there's the room with the giant bed and tiny cradle, both empty. I like this room. The sheets on one side have been disturbed—just on the one side. And on *this* side is a nightstand. Not much to see here, other than a book that appears not yet to have been opened—the bookmark sits on top; a digital alarm clock, a bottle of pills (sleeping pills, no doubt); a pen, a full glass of water (curious), and a photograph—here again is the departed family; they're older in this picture: the most lovely woman (who must here be in her early sixties), the elder girl (a daughter, holding what must be the grandson, her child), the scrappy girl (another daughter, sprouted like a weed), the infant (daughter number three, who seems to have taken Scrappy's place), and the boys (sons, surely, more strapping than ever, and all as tall as church steeples).

How happy they look.

How happy, indeed.

It makes no difference to me, really, where they went. I'm sure they have their reasons—*had* their reasons. I wonder what I had expected to find when I stumbled upon this place. Funny how something that had been so significant just minutes ago can simply vanish from the brain without a trace. I'm sure, if it really had been important, my reason, it will turn up in the old coconut.

Perhaps I had better take another look around.

Maybe then I'll recall my intentions.

Let's see now: I came here—*why*?

I don't know.

What had called me to this place?

I suppose it must have been the mystery of it all. How often does one stumble upon a house that appears to have been frozen in time, right in the middle of a perfectly decent, normal life. Though abandoned, I can see no real end in this place. It just *is*—no real beginning; no end; just stuck in the middle of *being*, kind of like how one feels when the realization of one's own existence can finally be recognized and recalled, that most curious sensation. It happened to me when I was five years old, and it's the oldest memory I have. One day I woke up in bed and everything felt brand new! Though the world and the baseline skills previously developed, like speech and walking, as well as names of people, places, and so forth, which had already been poured into the foundation, but without any sensational events to mark them—though these gradually came back to me as the day progressed, I was, for a while, quite unaware of who I was, where I was, and who everyone else was.

A foreigner was I, lost in my own body, mislaid within my own life.

There was no beginning, and I have yet to see an end.

Perhaps the end will be like the beginning that wasn't:

It will just be, and that will be all.

I've been all over this house. I can't remember why I came here; though, something, I don't know what, is calling me once more into the room with the giant bed and the cradle.

Sitting down on the disturbed side of the bed, I again examine the nightstand.

There's a drawer.

I open it.

I see glasses in a black case, a handful of mints (very thoughtful, whoever slept on this side), a Bible (interesting), and…

It's a folded piece of paper.

I take hold of the paper.

Unfold it.

It's a letter.

I can't imagine anyone will mind if I borrow these glasses—just for a minute.

Dear Departing One,

I haven't much time; neither do you. I must, for our sake, pen this while I still can. Heaven, help me.

I never thought I'd be here. I'm afraid—that's putting it mildly. If there is a mercy in all of this, it is that I know you, dearest one, have no fear at all. You should be just as terrified as I am; though, I know you cannot be so. How blind you are, how blissfully blind—do I even want to rescue you from this place? To let go, to say goodbye—would it be more a mercy to simply let it all fade away and not tear open the wounds with jogs such as this? How jarring it must be for you, should you even know, should you even remember.

No. I must not let you fade—not without a fight, however futile! You and I cannot let go with hands at our sides. Attend to this letter with great care. Read diligently, purposefully; extract every drop of meaning from my words. Listen. Remember. Hear my voice. Do not let this fall, as you are falling, into darkness.

Do you see that painting on the wall? The one framed in the handmade frame and coated in splotchy paint? Your son made that for you in the second grade, frame and all. It's of us—you and me, and him; we're playing baseball, his favorite sport. And there, on the dresser—there's the trophy your other son earned when he took first prize at Olympic Day. He gave it to you, immediately as it was given to him—a nine year old; he said you were the deserving recipient, as it was you who had made him strong: your little long jumper.

The scar on your wrist, the left one; look at it—that's where your daughter left a gash when you stood too close while she was excitedly excavating "gold" from under the backyard porch, gold you had buried there: those painted rocks from the brook, used to nurture her interest and make her feel as if she were a real explorer. The tiny, pink handprint on the wall—do you see it? Look at it. That's the one the explorer's little sister placed the day she discovered finger painting. You just couldn't bring yourself to wash it off, or paint over it. Don't you remember? We had intended to do so, but it was so small, so very tiny; it reminded you of the day she was born, when she gazed up into your eyes and placed her brand new hand upon your chest. That same handprint was painted upon your heart that day; the one on the wall is its external copy: a memory.

Do you see that crib in the corner? That's where your grandson sleeps when our daughter, your precious firstborn, drops him off for weekends with grandma and grandpa. Can you see his face? His name is yours. One day your daughter may wish to tell you why she had decided to name her child thusly; and when you hear what she has to say, you will, as I did, fall to your knees and weep such wonderful tears—you should. You did once.

I am losing you, dearest one; and I fear you may have already lost me. If you are reading this in the manner in which I fear you are, then it may truly be too late. But I must try. I must fight against the inevitable. I cannot accept this—who ever could? To sit here, helplessly, and watch you slip away; it is agony! Is there no way back?

How curious, indeed, this letter. And how emotional its author must have been—what remains is speckled with tiny, rippling dots that have bled the ink.

There can be no victory. All will fade away. Hear me, dearest departing one; hear these words as if they scream to you from here upon the page: I am afraid. I am so terribly afraid, and I am not prepared for any of this; but I will not sit here and recall to you that which even the world will forget—your name, your situation, your successes, your failures, your stockpiles of gold, your stores of knowledge. No, all of that will pass, as will the dust of your bones. What I can tell you—all I can tell you, that which I must tell you; that which you must never forget, no matter how weak, no matter how distant, you become—is that you are, even now, upheld in powerful arms: Arms of Love; arms you do not deserve; arms that have held you in your best, in your worst, and in every other time in between. And though you soon will crumble, these arms will never forsake you. They hold you even now, though you have forgotten their touch, and they will hold you even unto the end. Take comfort in their warmth. Take shelter in their strength. And do not let the fear that binds me bind you. It is in you, this fear; though, you know not why. Oh, that I could release it before you and I become one, that I could find peace before I become numb to all feeling, before the frigid, nameless wind corrodes from within your oblivious mind, body, and soul.

I must cease. Forget me, as you most certainly will. But keep them always in your heart. Tomorrow, as today, a stranger will you meet; and that stranger will you become and will you be when into the looking glass you peer, once the silent fire has seen through its work, and there find only you and never me.

Your pictures, trophies, scars, imprints, and your name—they will live after you, but not for long. Yet, those arms will keep you, forever. Indeed, they will keep you, as they have kept me and will continue to do until I fade forever into you, and you fade forever from me.

Goodbye, my dear departing one. May you know a little longer the arms that hold you now, and forevermore those that always will.

Yours Truly,

Perhaps I should not have read this—seems personal. Though, whoever vacated this place and left it behind must not have found it worthy of toting. Or, perhaps, they'd never found it. Maybe it was meant to have been—

Oh!

Now I know why that woman seems familiar! I saw her just the other day! Or, was it this morning? Or, last week? Last year, maybe? She was following me; at least, I thought she had been.

Several times I glanced over my shoulder and caught her gazing at me. At first (as I suppose any man would), I felt rather exhilarated; my ego enjoyed quite a boost, for yours truly had caught the eye of a most elegant woman! Not bad, brother—you've still got it! But I soon began to think she might have mistaken me for someone else. I began to register her gaze as sorrowful, desperate, hopeless; she appeared to be holding back tears. And then she called to me—I'm sure it was to me. She called a name I did not know. Obviously she had mistaken me for another man—her son, perhaps? Her husband? I cannot say. How curious, though, thought I, that she would follow me for as long as she had and *still* believe I was somebody else.

Oh, poor woman!

I do most sincerely hope she is well.

Wait!

What was that?

Listen!

That sound!

I rush downstairs into the foyer, as quick as these old legs will carry me. My heart pounds as I step into the light pouring into the foyer—external light, shooting in, blindingly, through the opened door.

I am sure I had closed this door.

Mother always insists that I do.

While I do not fear my neighbors or passersby, never have, these days (what with all that has changed) some, like mother, have become rather skeptical of others, even afraid.

It seems, now, as I peer through the doorway, horrified, that her fears were justified. The sun burns brightly overhead, but on the horizon—framed between the rows of trees lining the main road, all set neatly within the doorway—there rises another sun. Its ascent is a noiseless one; and now I know the sound I had heard: it was a chorus of terrified screams lifted from around the world, sung to the tune of a steadily intensifying wailing from mighty sirens—a cry so powerful it now shakes and breaks the very foundations of the earth, as it has already this petrified heart.

The sun continues to rise, and I see that the hall in which I stand has been bleached white, stained by the flash that birthed this second sun.

I know what I must do.

There is not much time.

Though I am cemented to the floor—my eyes unable to detach from the sun as it rises through the air at an ominously sluggish pace, being chased by its thick, puffy tail, looking like a tadpole wearing a ruff—I am forcefully taken by the arm and yanked away from the hall.

There is no one here.

Who is pulling me?

Only the rising sun, the door, which I now see had been blown from its hinges and shattered into splinters; and me: a terribly frightened boy—none but these can be found amid the void.

The yanking force drags my trembling body into the adjacent classroom, where I, along with my peers, take cover beneath our desks. They're here, all of them; I can feel them, but only empty spaces under quaking desks meet my eyes. I look around for a familiar face, someone in whose eyes I might take comfort, knowing that we are meeting our fate together and not alone. But I find no familiar faces, only empty desks, beneath which tremble and cry the phantom emotions and desperate prayers of those I know well, and will soon surely lose—they are so loud I can nearly feel the heat of their dense auras and see the ripples they make.

Glass shatters all around me.

I am far too terrified to scream.

A deafening blast echoes through the space, and I collapse to the ground beneath the weight of the world, and fall fast asleep.

At last, I awake.

The smell of spring—blossoming flowers, fresh grass, brand new songs sung from the highest treetops, laughter from dancing children and emerging lovers, and jovial whispers from colorful, cool breezes—blowing in through the opened windows across from my giant, warm bed fills the room; and I take it in with a great inhale and let it fill my body to the brim with its joy and heavenly tranquility, before reluctantly releasing it.

How refreshed I feel! How truly rested! To what do I owe this gratitude for having had what must have been the greatest night's sleep this mind, body, and soul have ever known?

I see no one in this big room.

The opposite side of the bed is empty, so too is my grandson's cradle in the corner.

Oh!

Of course!

My sleeping pills! You glorious snooze-makers—thank you! And thank *you*—what's this label say? I had best get my glasses. Here we are. Much better! Okay, um, let's see—thank you, Dr. Travis, for having prescribed this wonderful...what's it called?

Oh, why do these words have to be so complex? What is this? "Done-pretzel," or something? Such strange names come out of the medical community, I must say. But, despite this bizarre moniker, one cannot deny its effectiveness—indeed, these worked so well, I just might order another ten bottles! Good ol' Dr. Travis!

Well, I guess I had better not doddle—today is shaping up to be a big day! Seems I have already dressed myself. Oh, well—sleeping pills are not without their side effects, right? At least sleep-dressing is an efficient byproduct of the blessed drug.

I make my way down the hall. How curious to have found this lovely house abandoned, and in so pristine a condition! Every room is finished, furnished, and every one warm and clean! When and why did its inhabitants leave? This room here, with the walls painted beige: it appears to be an office. There's a large desk, neatly organized; a bookshelf, stocked from floor to ceiling; and a single window in the corner with a cracked sill. This other room, the one with the plain, white walls: I would guess this one is a guest bedroom, for it has but one bed, upon which neatly folded and plain sheets have been placed; a nightstand with only a lamp and clock atop it; a single dresser, empty; and there are two windows in this room, as well—both circular in shape. And the room I have just left: it appeared to me to have been occupied shortly before my arrival. There was a child's drawing framed on the wall; a small, plastic trophy on a busy dresser; a cradle in the corner; a plastic toy miner's helmet with a flashlight, upon which is written in black ink, "My First Expedition with Daddy;" and a small, pink handprint painted on the wall.

Curious, indeed.

Where did everybody go?

As I descend the stairs, my stomach is filled with butterflies. I stop for a moment to fix the jacket and straighten the tie—my hands wring with nervous excitement. This is the day! From our meeting to here—it has finally arrived!

As I step into the hall, I see one of the party's members reattaching the church's door to its hinges—but who could pay a penny's worth of mind to such things? For there, to my right, just a breath away…there she is.

Oh, how elegant! How perfectly lovely! Stunningly gorgeous! Absolutely beautiful!

Standing like an angel caught up in the breath of Heaven, there beside an older man in a plain, black suit—her youthful face covered with a snow-white veil, her body draped in the purest silk: an unblemished dress for an unblemished, virtuous woman.

Oh, how I adore her!

Be still, my heart, else we might not live to know, serve, and discover this blessed wonder in the life-long manner that the desire and fascination with which she has so passionately infected us so urgently compels!

I step to her side as one gliding, upheld by the still, peaceful air between us. Gently, though I am exploding within, I take her veil and lift it slowly, revealing the arresting, outer display of her radiant heart. None can compare to her gorgeous, external visage, nor to the goodness of her soul, which redefines beauty itself.

Gazing deep into her eyes—eyes floating in a pool of the happiest tears and situated above the very smile that had, when first beheld, won this undeserving heart—I take her delicate hands in mine; and with the entire world bearing witness, as the overflow of happiness leaks over my cheeks, I proclaim to her the very words I had long ago prepared and yearned to say to the one I had been destined to love, to honor, and to serve; the one of whom, I now know, beyond any doubt, I am so unworthy: "I am yours, this day and evermore."

A tear falls the length of her reddening face, and as I watch it drift slowly to her chin, I am aware—I am aware as I feel I have never been before.

The world itself is proclaiming its color to me.

A wild rush passes violently through my body, as if I am a ghost with earthly feeling, standing on the rocks of an ocean shore as it empties itself through me and onto the land.

I am as if awakened by a dreamland plunge through the air—shaken, and still quite unsure of my surroundings, as well as myself.

I am as one pulled from the grave by the powerful hand of Life, and I gasp as if for the first time, like a babe breaking free of the womb, seeking the one he knows intimately, but has yet to see.

I am aware!

I am awake!

I am alive!

My eyes fall deeper into hers and I squeeze tight her delicate, aged hands.

She looks at me, hopefully.

"My dearest," I say, my words heavy with the revelation of the ticking clock readying to strike my final hour, pressing like a vice against the walls of my heart, "I will know you forever. Though I am gone, I *will* know you; for in my heart burns the fire you lit so long ago, when we were but children in a wild, unforgiving, and uncertain world. I will feel you all my days, here, deep within; and I will know you. No matter what happens," come forth notes of urgency, "take comfort that I am born by powerful arms, arms made strong by the very love you have bestowed upon this undeserving soul."

I take her head gently into my hands and kiss her, as I did upon the altar of unity many years ago.

"I love you, my dearest," I whisper, hoarsely, as tears stream from my eyes and over my quivering cheeks. "And I will *never* forget you."

Again I kiss her; and as she weeps silently, I embrace her, as would a drowning man at sea his life raft, and weep tears of parting sorrow.

Oh, Heaven—that I would never release her…

I don't want to go…

Please, don't let me go…

I know not how long she and I have been gazing at one another. She seems eager to query me about something.

A name is uttered, carried on a gentle voice, like that of a dove; she calls as to a partner slumbering long past his due time.

I know the name she speaks.

It's not mine.

It is the name this same woman had called the day I had caught her following me.

And it is the name signed at the bottom of the letter I found upstairs in this abandoned house.

This man—whose name she has called after me, whose hand

had penned the letter in the nightstand upstairs; he must be someone very dear to her, for she appears to have had been crying, and recently. Her face is still wet.

I back away slowly.

I see a woman and two men in the house.

"I'm sorry," I say, rather embarrassed. "I seem to have entered the wrong home."

They do not appear afraid of me, as I would most certainly be if strange man had mistakenly waltzed into my home. No, they instead appear sad, desperate, hopeless. They watch me with sorrowful eyes as I mumble a hurried "Goodbye!" and slip out the front door.

As I hasten down the sidewalk, I look back, only once; and there—standing in my wake, directly in front of the house I have just left, gazing at me as I speed into the distance—is a lovely woman. Though she is quite a ways back, I can feel that she is more beautiful than any woman I have ever encountered. I know not why, but as I prolong this glance at her, I feel as though my veins are burning, and burning in such an exhilarating manner that I cannot help but wonder why my gut, my bones, and my very soul feel as if I know her, and know her well. I sense her comfort, her grace, her virtue, her goodness; though, she is a complete stranger to me. How curious to feel the essence of someone I have never met, to feel her as if she is a part of me, as if she has always been a part of me: a special part, the name of which I cannot recall, but know through and through.

A chill ripples through my body, and I turn my back to her

and continue on my way. But, as I do, the sensation within becomes stronger; and I am now aware of something my mind believes is foreign, but my soul knows is familiar.

It halts me in my tracks.

It is a voice—an angel's voice, no doubt—whispering a promise to me, one never heard before today, but one I know, in the strangest of ways, has been with me for many years. It is a promise of undying love and devotion, as well as a wish of gratitude for something I have done, something I am. I don't know what this is; and for a minute, as a familiar, wonderful warmth chases away the chill, I consider looking back…just once more.

But I don't.

I must continue on my way.

Prologue: Token

HOW are you, dear reader? Well, I hope. Any less, and I'm not sure you'll survive the Connerian onslaught still to come; we've only just begun. Whenever Conners is left unchecked by professionals like myself—or those experts in white coats presently trying to persuade the state to have him forcibly returned to their custody, for the sake of all humanity—, one must be absolutely sure of one's physical and mental wellbeing, lest one be sucked into the throes of Conners' unstable mind.

"And what is 'stable?'" the Author has oft said to me—his manner in these times usually forecasts a cloud of bloviation on the horizon; in such storms, questions are traditionally oratorical and meant for his ears only. "Is stability of mind dictated merely by the opinion of man and the conventions he has set in place?" Again, not really asking; though, not *exactly* rhetorical; rather, he speaks in times such as these as one addressing a dense crowd of admirers, filling the folds of his brain from end-to-end and rapturously hanging on every syllable that breaches his lips. "On what has man ever been consistent? Have the minds of men ever found perfect harmony with one another? Or, does man even seek to sample the minds of men beyond the borders of his own skull? What of *them* does he know? How, then, can one call another '*un*stable,' when stability itself has in the histories and present actions of men proved to be out of mortal reach?"

I've heard rumors that the state will soon be issuing a reward for my employer's "safe-*ish* and speedy return" to their custody.

I suppose, if the price is right...

Anyway, returning to my opening query: How are you, dear reader?

You know, of all the common, everyday exchanges of language between human beings, salutations, I would argue, hold a fair amount of intrigue and offer plenty of mental food on which to nibble.

Why?

Well, in my experience, I have observed that we, when summing up our overall wellbeing at the onset of a meeting, are often neither correct nor perfectly honest.

While some may, for a variety of reasons, put forth a word that will hasten the conversation past the opening pleasantries—either for the sake of time, or stemming from a disinclination to be transparent on the topic—sometimes I wonder if we know we're not speaking accurately. Replies to "How are you?" are often so kneejerk; do we ever really realize what we're saying?

The most common, grammatically incorrect reply to the aforementioned question is, "Good."

"I'm good."

"I'm doing good."

Who by now hasn't heard the grammar snob's snotty retort?

"Nay, nay, and a harry *harrumph*!" sayeth the grammar snob. "Super heroes do good—*you* are doing *WELL*!"

WELL...how do *YOU* know?

While I am not one to let someone who declares upon the conclusion of a successful feat that they "did amazing" get away without my first and hastily spitting out of the corner of my mouth "amazing-*ly*", if a person tells me that they are "doing good," who am I to say that they are not presently feeding the hungry, tending to the sick, courteously managing their email "Reply All" usage, or decorously setting the new toilet paper roll in the "over" position?

No.

While it may be true that most have a bad habit of substituting "well" for "good," one must take care not to presume another's meaning in such a situation.

How, then, about "fine"?

Is fine the same as "okay"?

The latter suggests a sense of satisfactoriness; while the former, in point of fact, should be employed to describe excellence! When we refer to clothing or wine as fine, we speak of its high quality, its great worth; yet, when speaking of ourselves, we often imply that there is room for improvement. Fine, in this sense, may be the most honest, for are we ever *not* in need of some improvement? However, I often wonder if those of us who feel we are lacking are actually drowning in abundance, and should, therefore, employ the meaning attached to wines and attire.

Some may say "so-so."

Beware!

For this usually means they want to tell you why; furthermore, they may hope this answer will prompt you to actually *ask* them why.

If not so-so, a person may unleash a crisp and precise, can't-be-misconstrued, this-is-what-I-mean adjective, which, along with any sort of negative or near-negative reply to a question regarding one's present state of being, is a recipe for a much longer conversation, backing you into a corner in which you'll either be identified as the true friend that you are, or exposed, like the rest of us, as an empty inquirer.

There are also "great" and "super" and "splendid" and "tubular"—though, I can't recall when I've ever felt so like a hose that I just had to make it widely known.

I am quite certain that a thousand more synonyms probably exist for "well" that the mold-breakers will use when conversing; but the one that baffles me every time I hear it, either from my own mouth or the mouths of others, is "all right."

Like "fine," "all right" is offered, in every case I've encountered thus far, with the implication that things could be better.

But...but...how?

You just said you were "all right." If *all* is truly right, then what could be better? All the things are right! EVERYTHING is *LITERALLY* where it should be, operating at peak performance, producing optimal results; for, if any one thing was presently yielding any less than tip-top, it would be impossible to join the words "all" and "right!"

Man, what I would give to be all right! Though, I suppose, I *am* all right in some ways. When I compose with a pen, I'm all right. When I shake a hand, I'm all right. When I'm driving down the road, I'm all right. When I employ the creative side of my brain, I'm (so they say) all right. And whenever I debate the Author or see my line of thinking cross his, I am, absolutely, without a doubt, all right.

Interesting.

Well, I suppose this has gone on long enough, eh?

I do hope you're all right, dear reader; though, as it takes a certain level of insanity to compose books such as these (those of the Connerian variety), and a certain level of masochism to read them, I'll take my assumption of your wellbeing to be within a satisfactory degree of accuracy and keep you foremost in my prayers.

The second story in this series of seven, *Token*, presents its own take on what it means to be "all right," and the way in which perception and perspective can define it.

Our tale takes place in the summer and follows a recent college graduate, who, standing upon the threshold of the future she's worked so hard to create for herself, decides to take a seemingly harmless gamble, breaking out from the order by which she has lived, and seize a chance at a thrill unknown, before stepping back into her familiar, orderly world.

Born out of a single line was *Token*. Repeated twice in the forthcoming narrative, these words came to the Author as he walked home from the gym through a chilly, overcast morning in August of 2018; and by the time he'd made it indoors, the basic concept for the story had been organized.

As Conners told me, when it was decided that Ramblings Two would feature this tale, "There is a promise offered by the world, but are we wise enough to truly understand it?"

Dear reader, I give you *Token*.

Proceed!

Token

Token

LATE one night, as the clock ticked into the morning, chasing away the last of the fleeting good things that might befall the children of the night, there sat a lonely young man, leaning against the bar and gazing into distant worlds beyond the haze of smoke and noise, while his fingers tumbled idly about a twinkling, golden light.

A handsome man was he, to put it mildly. Silken hair fell just below his ears, sun-kissed and sandy; it seemed to play with the breezes cast by passing revelers and drunkards, but never once did a single hair forget its place or lose a step in the dance. His features were by expert hands carved from the smoothest marble, chiseled with the utmost care: a thick and powerful jaw, with a subtle but most expressive cleft in his chin, so much so one might have noted its distinct personality; just the right amount of forehead wrinkles emitted age's most attractive features, though robbed him not of even a brushstroke of youth; and perfectly rounded cheekbones rolled and fell like a soft and soothing sigh into vales just deep enough to accent the hue of the even deeper oceans that churned within them, gracefully and compellingly, but not too deep as to be hidden beneath shadow—his offered the perfect dose of mystery to tempt the heart, a savory drop of flavor to electrify and starve the appetite. A most elegant suit adorned his shapely frame, complementing every curve, every peak and valley, leaving little to the imagination, but leaving the imagination little with which to be satisfied…or the intrigue to be quelled. He was the type of person of whom one would most likely take note when passing by, but of whom little more than the first-mentioned descriptor might be said when later called to mind. However, this night, this man was beheld by not just anyone—he was beheld by *her.*

All her life, there had been naught but her own tale upon the lips of the world—a condition paradoxically unique to no one. And, so, what her captivated eyes beheld—tasted through the hungry pores of her heightened skin, and felt deep within the one place undoubtedly more discerning and wise than what lies wasted between the ears—was indeed accurate to its true nature; and, thus, a valid perception. This sensual sensation before her, she knew, was exactly as only she could describe him.

She knew; therefore, he was.

But, oh, foolish head! How acquiescent you become before the bottle! Or, is it after*? Too ready to follow your own lead, and listen not to the heart! How like a fool you would be to believe! What is he to you, anyway? What are you to* him*? What are* we*? What is anyone, for that matter?*

Thus spoke the drunken philosopher into her glass—though, perhaps in a more concise phrasing, incorporating fewer flowery forms and fashioned in an order worthy of the name only if affixed to the prefix *dis-*. One would be hard-pressed to say for sure, for indeed the bottle brings forth foreign figures and peculiar personalities, known not to the mask of day; additionally, words muffled and bubbled into liquid are pretty darned difficult to discern—but that's neither here nor there.

And, so, another glass she poured, and toasted to whatever by this time remained, having toasted already to and thoroughly spent health, wealth, friendship, good fortune, and time.

A familiar arm arose under her own and began guiding her

through a maze of tables, chairs, and bottles as broken as the futures over which their contents had this night been spilt, back toward a shuttle that would carry her to headaches and regret. And as she staggered, her glazed gaze fell once more upon the man at the bar.

Twiddling still that twinkling, golden light about his fingers, he flooded the air with deep and soothing tones; and to a long-haired, high-heeled perfume explosion, with stupid cat-shaped pendant earrings of silver, a mouthful of perfect pearly whites, and expensive fingernails—to this vision before him, he cast forth a smile so rapturing, she hardly noticed how annoyed she was that his other hand was at that moment warming the dainty paw of a woman other than herself.

***

Headaches and dry heaves—another Saturday-night-turned-Sunday-morning was in the books.

Emerging finally from her bedroom, mere seconds before the morning became afternoon, she shuffled slowly into the hall. The previous week, she had left for a night out without closing the shades; even to the present day, she could not be totally sure it had actually been daylight streaming through her windows that next morning, and not, rather, a fiery freight train breaking through the glass and barreling over her, as she crumbled into a ball, squealing and squinting in pain.

Having thoroughly learned her lesson, she had made sure this week to leave her sunglasses beside the bed before departing; donning these, she walked into the hall relatively steadily and without fear of the light. She might have better learned her lesson by simply shutting the shades before leaving; but with all the recent cramming and non-stop studying she had been doing, some logic was bound to become misplaced.

It had been a long and difficult, but wildly successful, run: a golden tassel and a golden MCAT score, each received within one week of the other. She had told herself that nights like the last and the one prior were for celebratory purposes, and necessary, for soon her life would be turned upside down, more so than it had already been. Studies and long hours of intense work lay ahead; she needed a bit of a pre-unwind: an advanced de-stressing, before the world began moving again at a mile a minute, and then some. But, after last night, she felt that perhaps a hot cup of tea and an old movie, while wrapped to the neck in her bed comforter, would have proved far more effective to that end.

Still, these were special occasions. One week, she's jumping around the room with an exceptional MCAT result in her tightly clenched fist; the next, she's graduating with highest honors. The possibility loomed still for one more momentous event to usher in another night of celebration. If indeed the rule of three was at work in her life, and could be used to predict what might lay in the offing, she would this week open her mailbox and there find an envelope with the name of her desired medical school printed in the top left corner; and there, inside, her shaking hands would clasp down upon a letter bidding her welcome to a dream.

Oh, if such fortune might befall! Talk about hitting nothing but net! Her chances were, realistically, just as good as any of her accomplished peers. However, bubbling to the top was a hearty dose of confidence, mixed with a healthy serving of hope, and a pinch of pure, unbridled assurance that her run had been so calculated and so well-executed that there would be—could be—no misstep, not now.

Life can be unfair…but not *that* unfair.

Having poured herself a cup of coffee, she shuffled back into the hall (a bit quicker and steadier than when she'd first entered it) and out to the main lobby to retrieve the morning paper.

Part of her had hoped the mailman might have been taken by ambition and had decided to get a head start on Monday's mail by delivering today what even he had not yet received. Perhaps, thought she, there would be a letter of acceptance waiting for her in her box—or, perhaps better yet, a quick and clean, bandage-ripping rejection letter. Forget the golden tassel and the MCAT; *this*, in her book, was the big one: the one upon which all her attention was fixed; the one that had birthed all of her anxiety; the one that had been the very fuel that had driven the success of the latter two. And like a swift and terminal neck break following the short drop and sudden stop journey of the condemned, a definitive "No" delivered sooner rather than later, she felt, would be far more bearable than weeks and weeks of dangling.

Alas, she found nothing more in her mail slot than the Sunday paper.

President Accidently Thanks Deceased Man for Vote

Two Shot on Lower East Side

Disappearances of Three Women Connected,
Says Sheriff

Rising Star, 27, in Critical Condition
Following Overdose

Denim Dye Linked to Cancer, Study Suggests

Struggling Ball Club Loses Seventh Straight

Unusually Cloudy Summer Linked to Depression,
Experts Say

These headlines didn't exactly put the "sun" in Sunday. Hopefully this wasn't foreshadowing for the rest of the week.

Bleak as things might have been beyond her door, there was plenty of good headed her way—she just knew it. This week, she would surely hear back from the college; she had, of course, been waiting patiently for so long!

Yes.

Yes, indeed.

This was the week.

She would finally hear back on the status of her application.

She would hear back, for sure.

And she would…yes; she *would* be accepted.

Accepted…

Accepted!

And, who knows?

Perhaps that rule of three might just have in store a bonus number four.

***

Summer days came, and summer days went, each leaving a warmer impression than the last. Cloudy though it had been, it seemed to her that there cut through the haze a ray of sunshine greater and brighter than the one that had cast away the shadows the previous day. Yet, brilliant though these daily displays were, each would eventually be taken by the clouds when came the inevitable night. These were exceptionally cold nights; only the company of her friends had banished such frigidity in the past. But those soothing voices and loving embraces had for the summer months flown south, flown east, and in every other direction—some, who like her had graduated, had departed for good. There was now no one to warm her lonely nights. Ice cream was her only nightly companion, paradoxically providing what warmth her soul was lacking—as best it could, at least.

"No, really—I'm all right. You don't have to—I know, but—Mom...*Mom*! Honestly! I'm a big girl! It's just one week more, then I'll be—No, she left two days ago. I'm totally fine; I've lived alone before! Mom…it's not forever—just one more week. My replacement couldn't start until *next* Monday, and they've been so good to me these past few years, I didn't want to leave them short-handed. Yes, I'll be on the road first thing *next* Saturday morning. One week, Mom—that's it! And then your little girl will be home! No, no, no—I won't let you do that. You guys made the trip last week, and I won't make you do it again. Don't feel bad about it! Now all my stuff is at home waiting for me! I can just load up what little I have here, hit the road before mid-morning, and be settling back into my room after the long drive, without having to do any real unpacking! Really, Mom,

I'm fine with the air mattress; it's more than enough for now. I don't need the couch and stuff for this last handful of days. Of course she took her furniture! Did you think she'd leave it behind just for me? Okay, I'll admit, I should have called the second plans changed; but it has just been so busy. Mom…I've got a TV, an air mattress, a pillow, Mr. Teddy Buns, a whole pint of Vanilla Cherry Swirl, and plenty of plastic spoons with which to eat it—I'll be fine. No, Mom—those aren't gunshots; I'm walking down the stairs. I'm sure they're structurally sound. Yes, Mom…this neighborhood is safe. Don't you remember? You called it a page right out of the '50s? Well, sure, I mean, *of course* they had crime in the '50s, but…oh, never mind. By the way, did you and Dad ever…Oh, my gosh…Mom—*yes, I'm still here*—Mom! I GOT IN! The college! The college! I got in! It just came! Today! *Really*! In my mailbox—where else? Mom! I'VE BEEN ACCEPTED!"

***

All things come in threes…until they come as just one, or include a fourth.

Three monumental things had happened to her, each taking place one week from the other over the course of three weeks. She had earned an exceptional score on the MCAT, had graduated with a golden tassel, and now she had been accepted to her primary choice medical school. Had she any money, she might have considered picking a few racehorses or trying her hand at the local riverboat.

She had been on the phone for the better part of the day with friends and family, weeping and screaming, shuffling through all the joyful emotions, until, after all the dialing and relating the same, super-amazing story to countless loved ones, she was physically and emotionally exhausted. But that was, as they say, A-Okay; some sort of luck or good fortune seemed to be on her side.

Her heart had been sprinting and flipping and dancing all afternoon, and her jaw would just not stop quaking. Placing her phone delicately atop the kitchen counter, she, with her last burst of energy, clenched her fists, gritted her teeth, and as her eyes sealed tightly and her whole body contracted and shook, she let the power streaming through this newly-opened door in her life sink through her every pore, until she had become so infected with ecstasy that the euphoric shout building in her chest could no longer be contained; and, exploding into the picture of a leaping starfish, with her head pointed to the sky and her every limb extended to full length, that triumphant, exhilarated cry bellowed forth and danced about the walls, maintaining its buoyant energy long after her wind had been spent.

Her body pleasantly drained, she floated like a falling leaf from her elevated position among clouds, plopping gently down atop to the kitchen counter, her legs dangling freely over the edge.

Sitting in the silence of the empty apartment, she gazed at the bare walls and vacant spaces.

A sigh trembled past her lips.

How she wished her mother could have been here as she'd opened the letter—if even her roommate, or someone special, had been here to share a hug; that would have been nice. It was such a big thing, and she had only herself and the voices coming through her phone with whom to experience it. Her lips tightened; and though she was alone, she fought to forbid that growing tear from tumbling toward her cheek.

This would not do.

No, this was a night for which no amount of ice cream or old, black and white mystery/romance films could do any good whatsoever. All of her friends had gone home; there was no one familiar nearby to call, and certainly no alcohol could be on the menu; but she had to be around people. Perhaps the energy of a crowd could help to soothe her nerves.

And, so, without a second thought, she made a dash to the bathroom, gave herself a quick dolling (nothing too wild; just something to cover the emotion and make her a shade or two better than presentable in her own eye), threw on a cute but comfortable top and jeans, and headed out for the town.

Half a step through the doorway, she realized she'd forgotten her purse.

Snatching this from its usual place, she commenced Exit: Take Two.

And as the door slammed behind her, a call came through on her cellphone.

It would vibrate for a few minutes more, there, on the kitchen counter.

***

The setting summer sun was on full display, but the lights of the main road cast over it the same cloud that suffocates all stars.

She had walked from this place to that one, sampling what revelry was taking place, or preparing to do so. Without alcohol, things seemed a lot less interesting. Her last few nights out on the town had been her first in some time; and she wondered now, as she observed through glasses of sobriety, if indeed anyone had ever had an interesting or good time in this place and places like it. What fun had been forgotten was, perhaps, not much fun at all. How anyone, including herself, could be fooled so regularly by such a blunt and brazen deceiver as the bottle seemed so simple and incomprehensible a query.

In and out this door and that one, again and again finding variants of the same old song and dance, the one seen so pleasantly and humorously on television, but rather pathetic in practice: this had become the night's main act, stuck in an endless encore. She found herself a bit nauseated by the whole show, and things did not improve as the hours ticked.

Not one to forfeit so easily, however, she decided to give the night one last chance, and entered through the doors she had exited under the power of another's arms exactly one week prior. And, to her great surprise, she beheld, in the exact same place as before, the young man that had been the fixation of her attention for an entire night, as well as a mental fragment floating about in ignorance for the last one hundred and sixty three hours. But she knew him at once; that fragment was instantly snatched into vivid memory.

He was almost exactly as she had remembered—this time, however, donning a different (though, still dashing and sophisticated-looking) suit, complete with the tailored pants, wholly wrinkle-free shirt, and jacket seemingly woven onto his body from the locks of angels. His hair was just as long and silken, just as sun-kissed and sandy; his jaw was so powerful, she quaked slightly; and so expressive was the cleft in his chin, she could almost hear a story of great mystery being told through it, as only it, with its distinctive personality, could tell. His forehead wrinkles accented his youth with a song of dignity and maturity, as if they were the stings of a vibrant guitar singing melodies of old. The roundness of his cheekbones had not been an invention of the mind, nor had the blueness of his eyes, set deep within their vales, been the product of wild dreaming. And about his fingers, surely as before, twinkled a silvery light.

And that smile…

How could she have forgotten that smile?

A bite-sized version was lifted to the bartender as the young man's glass was refilled; deep within, she felt a twinge of jealousy.

What might it be like to be the one at whom *that* smile is directed, she wondered? How much more might a full smile knock her to the floor?

She remembered the silly woman he had entertained last week.

Where was she now?

Just a flash in the pan, perhaps?

I'll bet, thought she, that he'd seen right through her.

I'll bet her fast-paced, flirty, frivolous intentions didn't match his own—surely of nobler quality.

And now he's back here, alone.

And she's nowhere to be found.

Now seemed to be as good a time as any to take action. Though she had entertained the thought of romance many times before, there had for her never been any real effort to entertain or invite it. Her studies and successes had always been at the forefront of her mind, leaving little time for romantic relationships. But these past two weeks had been an adventure into the new. She had gotten drunk—*twice*! That was new. She had "partied" until after midnight—*twice*! That was new, too.

Could this be the next new adventure?

The last two new adventures had been carried out with little thought; she had basically allowed the excitement of the moment and the energy from her friends to break down her inhibitions, and thereafter partake in something she felt would be practically harmless to her future and goals. It wasn't like drinking and partying a little bit was some crazy thing only a few social outliers did. Harmless, indeed—under the proper regulation, of course. But this would be different. This would be human-to-human interaction and contact.

Even without a drink, the possibility of drunkenness loomed; she assumed a human hangover would be far more difficult to expel than one found at the bottom of a bottle. But she feared a different kind of damage: one she had witnessed in all the movies and a handful of unfortunate friends; a damage of which she could but speculate regarding its translation into real life; a damage she was in no hurry to experience.

On the other hand, thought she, this could actually be the ideal scenario. First of all, she would, in one week and for good, be vacating this town, leaving little room for any long-term consequences to come out of whatever might or might not blossom from this night. If there was to be any awkwardness—or, Heaven forbid, if he turned out to be some sort of creep—she'd be gone, and he'd be a distant memory. Just be sure, she told herself not to be too candid; perhaps she'd even offer a phony name.

Secondly, one week seemed like the perfect amount of time

to get in some practice—again, with little negative consequence. She had always dreamed of some day finding that fairy tale "true love," or some adequate reality; but, with no prior experience, she feared she might not know how to properly field that love when finally Life batted it her way. Life can send one some pretty crazy line drives, and one must be ready, lest one let the line-drive of love sail into the distance, into the arms of another—or worse: straight and true into one's face for a broken and bloodied nose, or black eye. Perhaps now was a good time to break in the glove.

But then there was that other factor: what if all the stars aligned and this turned out to be something? What if this night melted into a wonderful, magical night? What if she found herself at the end of the week wishing she didn't have to leave? What if she started to conjure and entertain preposterous ideas, like forfeiting all she had accomplished to stay near this person?

No.

This is all crazy talk.

When *ever* had she been so taken?

When *ever* had she been so helplessly and stupidly out of control?

People meet every day, she thought! Relationships start and end, succeed and fail—but this wouldn't even be that! *This* would be just two people sitting at a bar and chatting.

Her feet quaked as she moved to lift them from their stagnant positions and into forward motion; but there was a terrible sinking feeling in her heart. She realized now that it was very possible she had found the strength to embark on her past adventures only because her friends had given her the necessary push.

This was her first solo test, in many respects.

For some reason, she was hesitant to approach this young man—but, why? She had never before felt romantic rejection—was *this* the cause of her reluctance? Maybe she was afraid to know she might not be a welcome sight in his eye, and be plagued thereafter with wondering and desperately seeking to identify what about her is so repulsive. Or, perhaps she was afraid to find out he really was something special. Maybe she was afraid that her heart would open, that he would be inadvertently—or worse: eagerly and irreparably—invited inside. Maybe there was something even more substantial: a great compromise she might let herself make in a moment of rapture; an urgent acceptance of a deep etching, writing on her very being something that can never be erased; a willful, thoughtless forfeiting of something precious and vulnerable that she could never get back. What if he was perfect, a match, something she would want even more than everything else she had worked so hard to get, even so much as to cast medical school into the dust, only to be a barkeeper filling his glass that she might collect those bite-sized smiles? What if he would turn out to be her wonderful monkey wrench?

How ridiculous.

No man is so wonderful, she reasoned.

And so what if he is! I've got things to do in my life! And if he can't get on board with that, tough!

But, still—this won't be a relationship! Just two people sitting together and having a conversation.

That's all.

Nothing more.

Some people require (or, believe they require) some sort of liquid confidence. But with no designated buddy tagging along, and no history of shrinking in the face of opportunity, there would be no fuel other than her own will to carry her. She had made up her mind, and she was confident that, so long as she remained sober and among the public, she could control the trajectory of this night and learn whether this guy is really as good as he looks.

A solo adventure lay just ahead.

And, so, taking in a great gust of air through her nostrils, she waltzed directly to the bar, head high and chest pronounced.

She had never been the initiator in this kind of scenario—it was exhilarating! If nothing came of what was about to go down, this adventure would not be remembered as a bust. Every step landed atop a cloud, and the air rushing through her hair and swirling about her body carried an intoxicating aroma, the same one that would fill her to the brim every time she would clasp a firm hold of Life's reins and steer toward yet another triumph. The last two weeks had been celebrations of two such triumphs, and in those celebrations she had emerged even more from the shell she was slowly discovering had all her life surrounded her. And now, on another such night of celebration, sitting before her was yet another chance to shatter the shell she had become convinced was in need of a swift breaking.

"Is this seat taken?" she purred, gliding to the stool before the young man and plopping one hand down atop the bar.

She could feel the breeze blowing through the bar's open door teasing the ends of her hair, and she could just see herself glowing like a movie star as she leaned against her hyperextended arm, while her other hand glided lazily over the barstool, balancing precariously on the tip of her finger, tracing aimlessly over the glossy wood. A not-so-small part of her felt completely ridiculous, speaking as she had and reveling in the thought of how she hoped to (but was certain she did not) appear in his eye; and yet, while it wasn't exactly a rush, it was, as she would later reflect during the course of the night, fun—almost, thought she, the same brand of fun had as a child while playing dress-up.

The young man's eyes, which had been fixed upon the silvery light dancing about in his hand, casually looked up, piercing her with their deep, icy blue.

"If you like," he hummed, gazing intently at every feature on her face. "But, I must warn you," he added, as her body twitched forth, "I'll be the worst mistake you'll ever make."

To be perfectly honest, this line knocked her a bit off balance, and was accompanied by the door of the bar slamming shut and the breeze instantly ceasing to blow.

She felt as though the reins had been violently yanked from her hands.

A silent, interminable moment or two later, a tiny smile grew out of the corner of the young man's mouth. Warm though it was, it could not banish the deafening chill running down her neck.

She drew a deep breath, a large chunk of her attention fixated on concealing her doing so.

He broke first the gaze, shooting his eyes onto the stool, then back to her.

Quickly regaining her confidence, she took up the reins once again and sat down, intent, more now than ever, to play the game to win.

"I'll be the judge of that," she replied, floating into the seat.

"And what might be your name?" came a deep and soothing, soft and warm voice from behind barely parting lips.

So elevating was the intrigue of this adventure that she found herself hovering high above him, so much so that she worried her answer might not have reached his ears. His reciprocal introduction met hers, however, loud and clear; and, moments later, she realized their hands had joined.

"This is a lovely ring," he said, clutching her hand by her fingertips, and gently massaging with his thumb her transparent glass Claddagh ring. "Right hand, heart pointing toward your fingertips—does this ring tell an accurate tale?"

Though she knew that ring by heart, as it had been gifted to her by her mother on her sixteenth birthday, and she had worn it in the same manner ever since, she dropped her eyes to it, just to be sure.

Indeed, the arms that formed the ring held the crowned heart as if in offering, with the heart's base pointed toward the fingertips on her right hand.

She nodded.

"May I buy you a drink?" he asked, speaking with an inflection that affected her as a live electrical wire striking her chest.

His massaging was like a numbing trance; it threatened to again steal the reins.

Politely refusing, she slowly slid her hand from his grasp.

"A soda, perhaps?"

What was she, *nine* years old?

She shook her head, but quickly forgot why she was doing so.

Deeper into his eyes she gazed.

"Water, then?"

Again, she shook her head.

This seemed to be the only thing she knew how to do; she could not recall for the life of her what query had prompted this reply.

"What can I offer you, then?" he asked, leaning back slightly, still twiddling the silvery light, and regarding her amusedly and with a look of mild fascination.

She sat very still for a moment, gazing yet into his eyes. A strange sensation began to take her; she worried her mouth might be hanging open, but she knew not which muscles to call upon to close it.

Then, she felt as though her phone had just vibrated in her pocket.

Subtly running her fingers along her thigh, she experienced a quick and violent moment of cold dread; she had left her phone at the apartment.

Regaining her focus, she saw the young man's eyes had diverted slightly, and had begun to watch her hand as it glided along her thigh.

She cleared her throat, and his eyes returned to hers.

"A conversation," she said at last.

The young man ran his hand through his silken hair and smiled that broad and rapturing smile she had seen the day her eyes had become acquainted with him.

"*That*," he said softly, pushing away his drink, "I would be honored to offer."

And as the echo of his words dissipated into the recesses of sensation, wherein lie the scent of the rose, the taste of wine, and the power of the gale as it wraps the body in a swirling embrace, he repositioned himself in his chair, then carried his twiddling hand to his wrist, where the silvery light disappeared behind his cufflink.

***

"Enough about me—how about you? What do you do?"

His was a rather tough act to follow. How he had done it, she could not say; to put so much into so little seems impossible. Yet, she felt she knew him—practically everything about him, she felt, had been conveyed. Perhaps not in so many words, but conveyed nonetheless. It was the *way* he had said it—no, it had been the structure of his story that had…well, no; it could have been the story itself: so interesting, so intriguing; a short story with enough meat to fill a novel, stuffed into only a few pages, leaving its reader craving just one more turn, just one more paragraph—just one more…something.

And now it was *her* turn?

Who is this "you" he'd mentioned?

And how was she to know what to say about her?

"Me?"

The young man but smiled and sipped his drink.

"*Me*—right!" she blurted.

Her eyes quickly scanned the lap of her dress, hoping there was, woven into the fabric, a personal biography she could recite.

A tiny flush of heat entered her heart.

"Um, well," she began, still feeling a bit lost, as her captivated mind was yet a little turned around in the dense and dazzling forest of his story. "I'm a medical student—well, no I'm not—I mean, I *am*—that is, I'm *going* to be a medical student. I just got accepted—today, actually."

How she had managed to trot that tied-shoelace-version of speech into something that could, albeit barely, walk the path of coherency was nothing short of astonishing—perhaps, she considered briefly, *this* had been her greatest accomplishment to date.

She could feel a blush filling her cheeks.

But if anyone could will away a blush, it was she.

"Indeed?" coughed the young man, having too quickly upon hearing the news swallowed his mouthful of battery acid. With a glow and a glisten from watering eyes, he continued eagerly, "Why, this is cause for celebration! You mean to tell me you get accepted into medical school and you choose to celebrate by going out to a bar all by yourself? What kind of friends do you have that would allow you to do a silly thing like that?"

"The kind who've just graduated and have already gone home, I suppose."

"Goodness! Does this mean you've *just* graduated, too?"

"Oh…well, yeah. I guess so."

Much to her chagrin, a tiny blush escaped her watchful will, and had scurried into her cheeks before she could stop it.

"So many wonderful things, and naught but a stranger with whom to share them! Come, let me at least buy you a drink."

It did seem like the thing to do: have a drink and celebrate. But, no—she needed to remain clear-headed this night. Not only was she alone, this evening might also hold in store a thing or two she would be very disappointed to forget; or, at the very least, experience through the lens of a funhouse mirror.

"No, no—but thank you," she stated with, as she believed, equal parts placidity and stern resolve. "I really don't want to be drinking tonight."

"Probably best," he sighed, appearing disappointed, but not without understanding. Examining his own drink, he continued, "Perhaps I'd better cut myself off, as well."

"Had several already?"

"Three. This makes four."

"You must have a very good head," she breathed with an airy chuckle, while in her heart that flush of heat began to churn.

Throwing back the last drops of his drink, the young man sent the glass plummeting to the bar with a *clank*.

He then extended both palms toward her.

"These," he said, noting his hands. "These are the only good things I have."

"Your head is no good?" she said, chuckling again.

"Not nearly as good as these," he replied on the wings of an exhale, still holding his palms to her, apparently having missed the joke that had taken her.

Retracting his hands, he brought them to just below his chest line, and there submitted them to a rather intense examination; he seemed, for a moment, to have become lost, as if a lullaby of stories was from those palms lifting like a warm perfume, entering through his every, steady breath.

"My head is the troublemaker," he mused, carefully scanning the curves of his palms, while his fingers twitched lazily, treading the air like legs dangling in a bottomless pool. "These," he continued, his eyes lifting and then falling into hers, as would an autumn leaf over a sleepy lake. His gaze was magnetic; it was grave, weighty, and endless—that leaf sank through her still waters as if through molasses. "These are always here to get me out of it."

"Out of what?" she asked, speaking almost trancedly as she lost herself more and more in the deep, blue pools spinning lazily in the bellies of their vales.

"Trouble!" he laughed, and with such out-of-the-blue mirth it felt to her like getting hit in the face with a baseball bat.

Her tongue staggered silently for a moment, mimicking her head, until at last she found speech.

"Any particular brand?"

Though it had by the hands of timidity been formed, these words found the strength to lift forth from behind her lips when a rush of heat that had in her heart been slowly brewing whispered a thrill for the unknown that comes of Trouble. It had been Caution and Forethought—agents of the mind—that had dominated her desires and driven her feet. By their example, she had gained confidence in the sense of control; and now, perhaps it was time to listen to her heart, to follow *its* lead, if just for a little while. Trouble, Danger, Rule-Breaking: these her heart craved—and only *now* had this been realized! Perhaps, through him, his stories, she might know the thrills of such adventures, break out of her vanilla world, the way she had done but days ago, the way she would be unable to do again for quite some time once school began.

Listen.

Follow.

The heart speaks.

Her eyes, filled with the beating of her swelling heart, beckoned his reply and begged for his words to fill the eternal space between their bodies.

"A brand, I think," came what might as well have been a song, or the plucking of Spanish guitar strings, dripping over his lips, "from which someone like *you* might not escape unscathed."

Whether the song had suffered a vocal cracking, or the guitar a severed string, was irrelevant—this was *not* something she was prepared to hear, nor was she *ever* willing to take such a snide sentiment from anyone. Who was he or *anyone* to assume *anything* regarding her capabilities? Such a statement was bad enough; but it was that smile, the one that had accompanied his stinging words—*that* was what had really sliced through the mood, and proved it had indeed been no vocal or instrumental error or failure, but rather the soft click of the trigger attached to a flamethrower deep within her core, primed by his foolish flicking.

"Someone like *me*? What's *that* supposed to mean?"

Seemingly unaffected by her sharp and meant-to-feel-like-a-slap-in-the-face tone, he continued.

"You strike me as the cautious type," he crooned, appearing rather satisfied with himself, as if he felt he were on some sort of a roll; as if his flick had been a calculated one, "the kind of person who knows what she wants, or *thinks* she wants, and gets it by the book."

"Wha—"

"You're above reproach; it's your obsession to be so. That's why you never do things like this: approach strange men at bars. Going to medical school requires dedication and focus; and you're not the type to let success slip through your fingers. Success *will* be yours—yet, it must be attained *only* through a clean nose and unblemished record. That's a boring way to live."

"How *dare*—"

"No doubt as your driving record would attest, you've been obeying all the rules of Life's road—you think *that's* how one finds real success or happiness? How do you expect to get anywhere if you stop when the world, or society, or whomever else, tells you to stop? How will you know the rush of the journey if you always obey the speed limit? And to what great destination do you expect to travel on the roads someone else has already mapped? What kind of living is that? Traveling the same way everyone else does and is expected to do? You're no different than the millions of others who are born, exist, and die—you'll just have a bit more cash to leave behind, but not a memory worth taking."

There were a zillion words and combinations of words she could conceive to spew like acid at his infuriating smirk, but she had lost the power of speech. Her legs, however, were as good as ever. Operation Depart Before I Kill this Jerk promptly commenced.

"But," he added quickly, clasping her wrist as she shot to her feet.

She flung her arm from his grasp; her eyes like daggers plunged deep into the beautiful oceans before them—how she hated that she could not think of a nastier adjective to describe them.

"But," he said again, much softer than before and bending toward her, "you *did* come here tonight, didn't you?"

Her body leaned slightly toward the door.

"You tried something you've never tried, and you did it alone—no friends from whom to draw your courage."

One foot readied to depart; the other seemed to have just stepped into a bear trap.

"It's not like you, what you've done; you're out of your element. You didn't even need—or want—so much as a taste of liquid confidence."

Was the leg of her chair a boa constrictor, coiling about her thigh? Whatever was happening, her body could and would not be seeing the door just yet.

"I think," he sighed, as he slowly reclined, "that on some level, perhaps subconsciously, you've already come to realize everything I've said. If I had to guess, I'd say that cocoon of yours, however forged—I'd say you're finally starting to peel away at its layers and raze its walls."

Though she could clearly see his hands were nowhere near her body, and there was no one else lurking about, she felt as though someone had taken her gently by the shoulders and was guiding her back into the chair. And then, just below those deep, blue pools she had hoped to transform into deserts with her fiery glare, there grew a smile—not the same, smug type she had seen throughout this bizarre and rather abruptly introduced chapter of their acquaintance, but rather one of mild, sincere understanding; she felt as if she had become transparent to him. His face bore the very image her own emotions and most private thoughts had tried in whispers to convey to her brain, but could never fully materialize; he looked, to put it simply, the way she had always wanted a witness to her most sacred places to look when she, laid bare, had at last been presented.

"So, what do you say, butterfly?"

Slowly, gently, his fingers slipped beneath her palm.

She let them.

"You ready to spread those wings?"

***

"Wait! Wait! Wait!"

"C'mon! We're almost there!"

She tried to protest again, but her wind was currently employed in replenishing her lungs from the all-out sprinting she had just done, and supplying the uncontrollable laughter bellowing forth from her belly, only barely restrained to a whisper—they had to be quiet.

"Over here!"

"No! No!" she cried, giggling still and scurrying to his side.

"Up here! C'mon—I'll give you a boost!"

"*Shh*! Someone will hear us!"

"Don't be a baby! Let's go!"

"A *baby*? Excuse *ME*, sir!" she exclaimed in a hush. "Babies don't have the nerve to steal slushees!"

With that, she dove forward and took a giant *SLURP* from the jumbo cup in his hand.

"*GAH*! Brain freeze!"

"Serves you right!" he chuckled, taking a sip of his own. "But, to be honest, I kind of think that cashier just let you take yours—you were really putting the moves on him!"

Still holding her frozen head and dancing gaily about, as if such could ease the pain, she gazed up at him through a single, squinted eye, and said, "You jealous? I was just following orders—and I did a darned good job, too! He didn't even turn his head when the doorbell rang as you stumbled out of there."

"Maybe if you'd have taken something bigger than the kids' size, I would agree that you've got nerves of steel. But I'm not convinced! Now, get up here and prove yourself!"

"Fine! I've already done *one* illegal thing tonight—what's one more?"

With that, she chucked into the bushes the now empty cup she'd taken from the convenience store and stepped forward.

A look of barely contained laughter on her companion's face caught her eye.

She looked back at her litter.

"Okay," she laughed with a shrug, "*Two* things. Now, help me up!"

With a final swig from his jumbo cup, the young man tossed it into the alley, took her by the waist, and lifted her to the last rung of the fire escape ladder.

She giggled the whole way.

He could hardly contain his own laughter.

After several attempts and a great deal of sweat spent through his brow, her hands caught the ladder and held on tightly.

But she just dangled.

"Stop laughing and pull yourself up!"

"I *caaaaaaan't*!"

"Channel your inner superhero! You can do it!"

"I'm too weak, idiot! Help me!"

She was now nearly all-out laughing, on the verge of throwing caution to the wind, and worse: losing her grip and maybe breaking an ankle on the way down.

"*Shh*! Okay! Hang on a second!"

The young man darted down the darkened alley and returned a few moments later, pushing a dumpster.

"Gross!" she cried. "What are you doing?"

"I'm gonna put this under you—use it to step up!"

She did so, and began to climb.

Leaping from the ground, the young man clasped the ladder and climbed after her.

"I think I hear someone!" she whispered sharply down to him.

"Keep going!" he called back.

The cool, night air whipped about her exposed skin, but her entire body was so aflame she knew not its bite; instead, it gave her the sensation of soaring—she was flying up into the clear, midnight sky, soon to be above the city lights and among the glittering stars.

Body trembling with excitement, she at last reached the top, and with a moderate amount of difficulty pulled herself over the rooftop ledge.

She stumbled a bit at first; her feet had never been so high above the ground—indeed, she'd never even been on an airplane or rollercoaster to carry her feet this high; a grounded life had been hers until today.

Like a newborn fawn, she stepped cautiously on wobbly knees, terrified but determined to make it to the opposite edge, wherefrom she would feel the power of the city break upon her, wherefrom the view would be nothing short of—

"*Breathtaking…*"

"Isn't it?" came the wild and soothing voice attached to the arms that had just wrapped about her from behind. "It's the best view in the city."

It was as he'd said, and even more so than it could ever have been, or would ever be, in any other scenario—she knew this with absolute certainty.

"You'd think they'd have better security on this building. But, alas," he sighed, and whispered as his lips slid closer to her ear, his cheek brushing along the back of her neck, the invisible stubbles thereon sending tingles throughout her body, "the government's eye remains blind."

Her eyes wanted not even to blink; not one moment or *milli*-moment did she want to miss. And as they burned in the passing breeze, a tear tumbled forth onto her rosy cheek.

It was then, despite herself, that she sealed her eyes, pushing another tear down the opposite cheek; for it was all just so much, perhaps too much; yet, it was everything her heart could at the moment conjure to want. And, paradoxically, through veiled eyes alone could she hope to experience this rapture with total, sensual awareness, to truly feel the rush of this moment, the flood of emotion, the tidal wave of ecstasy that was washing over her. There, found at last in the shadows cast over her eyes, her heart was content in the unending hunger it had discovered.

When again she opened her eyes, she found the city to have become a far more grand and glistening spectacle than before, and the warmth of the arms that held her was to her of more comfort and security than a winter blanket warmed by a country fire.

She was alive.

She was ready.

Without further thought, she again sealed her eyes, turned 'round, and with her heart to guide her, found what had been waiting for her, there, beneath his deep, blue eyes.

One life was over.

Another would rise unto a starry dawn.

***

The bright lights of the park cast out the glow of the stars, yet barely lit the way.

Cobblestones underfoot gave the ears just enough to know if indeed the path continued toward the next insufficient light; and *click* and *clack* away she did, her feet hesitating not once to lift and fall, and do it all over again. Content was she; so assured of and confident in the arm upholding her, warming her, and keeping the hidden horrors of the night at bay, that whether ground was firmly beneath her feet or awaiting her next step made little difference whatsoever.

"I wonder what time it is."

"I don't," she sighed, nuzzling her head into his shoulder, as they *clicked* and *clacked* along the path. Pulling closer around her neck the jacket he had somehow peeled from his frame and placed onto hers, she imagined for a moment she was a supermodel on a runway, or a queen. "Who cares what time it is? Well, *you*, obviously—but I for one couldn't care less from now on what time it is, or will be. As far as I'm concerned, time can take a—oh, *hey*…"

The pair, having just passed beneath one of the lamps, came to an abrupt stop.

"What's the matter?"

"Your neck! Oh, my! That's a nasty scar! How have I not seen it before now?"

The young man let out a languid snort.

"Well," he grinned, "earlier tonight I had a button," and, taking her hand, he placed her index finger upon a buttonless collar, saying, "right *here*—that is, until *someone* got a little carried away."

"How did you get it?" she continued, ignoring his dismissal and placing her head nearer his neck.

Gently pushing a breathable distance between them, he, as

he had in the bar, held up his hands to her; light from the lamp reflected shades of silver and gold from beneath his shirt cuffs.

"Trouble," he said with a shadowy smirk.

And now, as she had not done in the bar, she fully regarded his hands.

How scarred they were.

"*Heavens…*"

Lowering his hands, he said with a heavy sigh, "That trouble-maker just above the shoulders has left a great deal of torn flesh in its wake. And I remember every story—perfectly."

"Every *story*?"

"Scars are what help us remember," he replied, slipping his hands into his pockets; "most often, they're the only way to recall the things that alter our respective trajectories. The scars that heal—*those* stories are forgotten, along with the ones with whom they were made; and, perhaps," he said in a tone hushed like a lullaby, though more electrifying than one thousand untamed volts, as his scarred hand slowly lifted from his pocket, reached forth, and, like a warm breeze, carried her hand into a secure embrace, "forgetting also the one who did the healing."

Though her heart was racing and her head swimming in a whirling vortex, she managed to craft and deliver with stability (and a touch of sultry spice to boot) a coherent reply.

"By that logic, and your apparent history of troubles," she purred, pulling him closer, "I guess I'll have to cut you pretty deeply to even show up on your radar."

What had been a shadowy smirk grew into a wide, tenebrous grin, nearly blending with the benighted leaves of the bushes behind him.

"I *know* you will."

***

Each tooth scraped louder than the last, and fell into place with an increasingly deafening *CLANK*, like the slamming of a metal door.

Having at last passed every ward, the teeth clicked in unison; and before the echo from the penetration had faded, she came face to face with a scene she had been so sure lay some time into her future.

"Dare I offer you some wine? Or, would you prefer water?"

"What?"

Words had surely slammed against her ears, but they had done so all at once and in a hurry, violently breaking her trance.

Standing now in the present, she found herself in a doorway, heels in a hall and toes dancing nervously upon a Welcome mat.

"Water," he repeated graciously. "Would you like some water?"

"Oh…" Her trance returned, but only for a moment. "Water…right—I mean, *no*!" Stepping slightly forward, she cleared her throat and offered a sheepish, "Sorry," before retreating back to the starting point and speaking nearly in a whisper, "No; no, thank you."

The young man, who had slipped halfway into the kitchen, halted any further progress and gazed at the young woman wearing his suit jacket and swaying in his doorway, eying up and down the opened door, and scraping the nail of one index finger with that of the other.

Letting out a sigh, he donned a tight-lipped, knowing smile, and walked slowly toward her.

Taking her cold, trembling hand in his, he waited; she

trembled all the more.

Another steady, warm hand then fell upon the blocks of ice attached to her wrists, and through the air sailed a soft, soothing breeze, the gentle sound of which formed gracefully into, "I suppose, then, I should offer you a ride."

What calming she had experienced for those few moments his words drifted delicately into her ears was then erased when the final word bounced off the eardrum and ricocheted into her brain, where it triggered a halting of the heart and widening of the eyes. And then, just as her jaw was extending, those widened eyes perceived the young man retrieve from his pocket a set of car keys, which he proceeded to jingle before her. What followed was a bout of laughter so compelling, she was soon unable to stand; its mixture—containing heaps of relief, several servings of nervousness, a generous dash of trepidation, and a pinch of good humor found in the look of realization upon the young man's face—yielded a rather potent brew.

Expelling residual giggles and wiping tears, the pair staggered to a nearby chair, in which he deposited her limp and weary body, and then left to retrieve the water to which she had at last agreed with a speechless nod.

With one last airy chuckle through her nose, she extracted her makeup mirror from her purse, and in it surveyed the damage, as she shook her head and inwardly chastised herself for having let nerves get the best of her. It had been a wonderful night, and through it all she had remained in control; nothing had happened that she had not explicitly allowed or initiated—and so would the night end, despite the teachings of storybooks and movies that make out this very place to be the tremendous conclusion.

Well, not *this* place, exactly—just one door further.

And it was that very door upon which her eyes had become fixed.

There, reflected in the makeup mirror, she saw what was behind her: a cracked entryway.

Why she was instantly compelled to act in so sneaky a fashion, she could not say; surely, there could be no action of which the young man would not take note, as he was but a few paces away, preparing a drink that normally takes but a handful of seconds to prepare.

Yet, she rose from the chair with haste and slithered quickly around the corner and through the partially opened door.

The room was exactly what she had hoped and feared it would be: his bedroom.

Knowing she probably had only a moment or two to gather as much evidence about whatever character traits and juicy secrets he had yet hidden beneath his charm, she stood very still and let her eyes dart about the room.

The bed was made—perfectly.

Several books were stacked atop a nightstand; their titles were too distant to be perceived.

The closet door was closed.

A collection of shot glasses with various designs printed upon them ran the length of an elevated shelf.

A lamp in the corner was lit; its design was that of a vintage movie-studio spotlight.

In the corner lay an empty duffel bag.

A whole other outfit—complete with shirt, pants, jacket, tie, and shoes—rested neatly over and beside a desk chair.

And there was a desk, boasting three drawers—and hanging

from the round, silver knob of the top drawer was a golden pocket watch, dangling from a golden chain.

There was no time; she should be getting back.

But it was so…interesting.

How often does one see a pocket watch, anyway?

Especially one so expertly crafted.

The outer rim was like a rope; the face of it was porous: smooth, yet with tiny depressions so faint they barely registered to the touch; and at the very center was a most handsome, golden flower, blossoming as no flower has ever blossomed: bursting with petals so vibrant and detailed, they seemed divinely carved. Such beauty—one could nearly taste its sweet perfume. And, lastly, the ring attaching the watch to the chain was of a swirling design, like rising, dancing smoke from the raging belly of a dying fire.

Taking it gently in her hands, she slowly caressed the timepiece, running her finger along the rope, gliding across the porous body, petting the delicate flower; and at last floating through the smoke…wherein she found a tiny button perched proudly atop a tiny base.

She had no intention of pressing it—knowing little of pocket watches, she feared this might be some sort of trigger for a wake-up alarm, or something else noisy and awful. Yet, touch it she did; and instantly the face of the watch burst open, falling forward to reveal the hidden clock face within.

Having nearly dropped the watch in the rather (as she'd perceived it) explosive moment, she shot a glance toward the door and remained perfectly still, hoping to gain some sort of idea as to where the young man might be, and if he had heard her snooping.

Thinking there might be no better time than the present to make an escape, she moved to replace the watch and scram.

But not before a quick glance at the face.

A ring of Roman numerals surrounded a set of hands with heads like teardrops. Both the numerals and the hands were like ivory, and they were set against a pitch-black abyss. Together, they read three o'clock, which was not the correct time; and it was at this moment she realized that the third hand was not ticking; it had stalled on IV. There, also, on the clock face, she perceived something in the abyss, something terribly concealed by the darkness.

The shape was indistinct, yet familiar; full of waves, peaks, and valleys it was. Near its base, a winding stream slithered, running in equal bursts to the north, then to the east, then south, before repeating; a sister stream swam below it, separated from the one above by a canyon of black. Other matching, mirroring depressions could be found as the eyes journeyed upward; but it was the terribly deep set of depressions at the center that stood out in a most paradoxically stark manner. These were the darkest spots in this abyss; and, floating somewhere further, deep within them, though she could not tell for sure, there seemed to float orbs of crimson.

But, above it all—though, also and oddly, least—was the twinge of fire that seared her gut when her eyes adjusted further, and she beheld her reflection in the abyss.

"You like it?"

This time, she did drop the watch—in fact, she chucked it, and with not a little vim.

She turned quickly, face white as a ghost's, to see the young man rising in the doorway, smiling and holding the pocket watch in one hand and a slightly upset glass of water in the other.

"Tell me you saw that!" he cheered.

"What?"

"I caught that! You didn't see it? You missed it?"

"I'm—I'm *so* sorry!" she blurted, nearly interrupting. "I shouldn't have—"

"It's all right!" he reassured her, handing her the water. "I invited you to my home—*this* is part of my home; so: Welcome!"

"Yeah, but I—"

"Whatever it is you did or might have done, consider it forgiven. I have nothing to hide, here—surely not *this* old thing," he said with a smile, closing the face of the watch and holding it up before his gaze, "else I would have done better than to leave it out in plain sight."

Holding high the chain in one hand, he cradled the watch in the palm of the other, and gazed at it as one might a newborn.

"No," he breathed, musing with semi-widened eyes; "no hiding this thing; yet, for some, what lies in plain sight remains invisible. It makes one wonder if anyone is even looking," he added with a chuckle. "Some things *want* to be found."

With that, he gently touched the button, causing the face of the watch to burst open. He then spun the base on which the button sat, revealing it to be, as far as she could tell, some sort of winding mechanism.

Spin it he did, but only slightly.

He then closed the face and handed it to her.

"A lovely piece," he said. "Though I wish I could say it had been passed down to me from generations upon generations of family keepers, I discovered it quite by accident."

"How?" she asked, sipping her water.

Smiling, he motioned to both the chair at the desk and the edge of his bed.

"Have a seat."

She floated down atop the bed; he took the chair; and, straddling it backward, he leaned over the chair's back and said, "This is a vessel of life."

"It's not a watch?"

This she said with a snort, as she pressed the button to open the watch's face.

The time had changed.

It was now four o'clock.

The young man gently extracted the timepiece from her hand, lifting it slowly by the chain. He then clicked the face shut, and let it swing freely just above the floor, dangling from his finger.

"Very observant," he chuckled. "Yes; it is a watch. But it has never told me the time."

"It's broken?"

"Not anymore."

Her heart had nearly hurled a giggle at this, thinking he was making some sort of joke. But then her ears replayed the very direct manner by which he had said it; matching this to the dour look that seemed to have momentarily come over him, she judged that a giggle might not be the most appropriate response.

She proceeded instead with, "How so?"

"It was once like every other watch," he said, carefully coiling the golden chain about his finger, raising the watch from the floor like a bucket from a well. "*Tick. Tock. Tick. Tock.* Round and round. Passing every number in its time. As expected. On schedule. As designed. *Tick. Tock. Tick*…it was broken."

She eyed him with tremendous interest and intently as she sipped her water; his words were like a day that sees the sun passed by cloud after wispy, grey cloud, while on the horizon rises a mass of darkness.

"But, I fixed it," he whispered, his smile widening as the piece grew closer to his face, which had descended slowly to the rim of the chair's back, his head resting upon his chin. "It was so simple. This little token, *ticking* and *tocking* away, with no one ever to take interest in the product of its work. So, I fixed it."

There was something in his manner that she did not like; he seemed to be twisting inwardly, ever so subtly. Perhaps the alcohol was finally getting to him.

"How did you do that?" she asked, speaking cautiously, but curiously.

His eyes lifted steadily to meet hers; his head remained still.

"A token," he murmured; and with that he rose slowly, spun the chair around, and sat facing her; then, he reached his fingers under the cuff of his right sleeve. Fiddling for a moment, he soon extracted a small piece of metal, which he then held before her.

As if instinctively, she reached for it—but he recoiled it into his palm, extended forth his other hand, and said, "Please; I must insist upon delicate handling."

She regarded his open palm, and then followed his gaze toward her glass of water.

Looking at him once more and for a few moments, she inhaled slowly, watching his deep oceans churn like midnight, icy waters.

Downing the last gulp, she handed him the glass.

Taking it, he set it upon the desk behind him, and then

promptly placed a tiny metal gear in her waiting, cupped palms.

Why he had been so insistent about *this* little thing, she could not say; but she played along, examining it carefully and trying to look interested.

It was a standard gear, the kind one would not be surprised to find in something like a pocket watch: small, circular, with a ring of jagged teeth encircling a five-pointed star, bearing a tiny hole at its center—ordinary; though, quite curiously, her fingers tingled when caressing its body.

"This," he said, pointing to the gear, "is a token, reminding me of the night I set this timepiece right, the night I breathed life into its crowded and confused body—the night I *un*made it, that it might truly be."

"Are we still talking about a watch?" she asked, regarding him through slightly squinted eyes; the shadows of the room seemed to be melding with his face.

The young man smiled warmly and lifted the gear from her hand.

"Of course!" he chuckled. "Listen to me—going on about my hobbies, as if they're at all interesting."

He stuffed the gear back under his cuff; and, after some fiddling, returned an empty set of fingers.

Having done this, he slid from the chair to the ground before her, took both of her hands in his, and squeezed them.

"This has been a most memorable night," he said, beaming up at her; a white glow surrounded his face.

She smiled back at him, and tried to reciprocate the squeeze he was giving her; for she too had had a wonderful night, and wanted, though she found herself struggling, to let him know it in a manner mirroring his.

"Perhaps," he continued, his voice like a choir of low, entrancing, echoing voices, "I can mark this night with a more permanent memory?"

As he spoke, his fingers fell gently over her transparent glass Claddagh ring, and began to pull.

Her heart leapt, pounding as never before—beating with such intensity it burned, causing a line of sweat to form along her brow.

Was this happening?

What was happening?

How could she stop this?

Did she want to stop it?

What was he doing?

Exhilaration coursed like a flooded river, breeching its banks, careening beyond control through her heart; it begged her to see this through to the end, while her mind screamed for protesting.

As the ring slipped over the knuckle, her head pleaded with her to do something, to close her fist, and maybe even use it; but her heart *had* to know, and her body could not for either form any reply.

Over the fingertip the ring fell and into the space between them, suspended over the ground by only his gentle grip. Then, as her heart slammed wildly against her chest and her head screeched like a boiling teapot, bellowing with such blazing intensity that she struggled to keep the room in focus, that gentle grip before her began to dance about the ring, turning the base of the heart that had been carved into the band in a direction it had never faced since it had been placed on her finger: toward her body.

It was happening.

Surely, *this* was happening.

Is this really happening?

Her heart exploded; her head fell silent; her body went numb; and she became lost in the dense and hazy air passing between them.

And then, just as the moment she had long awaited (but was unsure if she wanted just now) was about to unfold, she watched as his free hand reached toward the arm attached to the grip in which her ring was suspended, and sail to that arm's shirt cuff.

Unbuttoning it, he peeled back the sleeve, there revealing a black leather wristband, about which was wrapped a silver chain, running beneath what was like a series of belt loops. And attached to that chain, she saw several rings; and affixed to those rings, each to its own, she saw the tiny gear, as well as a golden necklace medallion in the shape of a lowercase letter "A"…and, lastly, a stupid cat-shaped pendant earring of silver.

And as paralysis took her, she watched as her precious ring was affixed to an empty ring on the gleaming chain, there to dangle among the others.

***

She had seen him from across the room. A handsome man was he, to put it mildly. Silken hair fell just below his ears, sun-kissed and sandy; it seemed to play with the breezes cast by passing revelers and drunkards, but never once did a single hair forget its place or lose a step in the dance. His features were by expert hands carved from the smoothest marble, chiseled with the utmost care: a thick and powerful jaw, with a subtle but most expressive cleft in his chin, so much so one might have noted its distinct personality; just the right amount of forehead wrinkles emitted age's most attractive features, though robbed him not of even a brushstroke of youth; and perfectly rounded cheekbones rolled and fell like a soft and soothing sigh into vales just deep enough to accent the hue of the even deeper oceans that churned within them, gracefully and compellingly, but not too deep as to be hidden beneath shadow—his offered the perfect dose of mystery to tempt the heart, a savory drop of flavor to electrify and starve the appetite. A most elegant suit adorned his shapely frame, complementing every curve, every peak and valley, leaving little to the imagination, but leaving the imagination little with which to be satisfied…or the intrigue to be quelled. He was the type of person of whom one would most likely take note when passing by, but of whom little more than the first-mentioned descriptor might be said when later called to mind. However, this night, this man was beheld by not just anyone—he was beheld by *her*.

Giving in at last to the dares pushed forth by her table of friends to do what they all wished they could do, had they not have already taken partners of their own, she rose to cast her line before the fish and see if he would bite.

After a few extra shots of liquid confidence and sprays of perfume, she smoothed her dress, tousled her hair, and started her strut to the other end of the bar.

"Mind if I join you?" she purred, having glided to the object of her challenge and leaned before him in as tempting a manner as she could muster.

The young man's eyes, which had been fixed upon a small something dancing about in his hand, reflecting the bar's dim lights, as if made of glass, looked up at her, piercing her with their deep, icy blue.

"If you like. But, I must warn you," he said, gazing intently at every feature on her face, "I'll be the worst mistake you'll ever make."

Prologue: What Will I Be?

DEAR reader, for this prologue, I have temporarily relieved my narrator of his duties, as what I wish to have said here and in the piece to come would be most appropriately delivered directly from me, rather than dictated through the hands of another.

Before I begin, I invite you to jump ahead and read the piece; let it speak to you, raw and unprepared, before I explain its background.

My goal in writing is not to please readers. While this is not to say that I hope *not* to please or entertain, I never approach the page or craft, or alter a story, with public approval or monetary gain in mind; nor will I declare an opinion in contrast to society's standard of acceptance or tolerance for the sole purpose of harvesting gain via the forging of socially-disruptive waves. Honesty is my pledge. I, therefore, have no issue whatsoever explaining how or saying bluntly that this piece is explicitly and unabashedly a condemnation of what I feel is today's greatest and even most celebrated evil: abortion.

Our world is presently one in which speaking one's mind is called admirable and brave, granted one's mind falls within that which is also called socially acceptable; and criticism of abortion is not by our emerging popular culture considered even tolerable—it is, in fact, condemnable. But Truth, however the world may wish to define it, is not bound by the boxes in which we hope to put it, the lenses through which we choose to view it, or the brands into which we seek to morph it. What is true is unchanging, infinite, and eternal; it is beyond our grasp, control, and ability to mold; no conception, notion, or desire of man can affect it in the slightest.

Instant access to ideas and voices through our numerous technological mediums has provided me with more arguments in favor of abortion than I had ever thought possible.

Not one do I accept.

Compound all the horrors and evils of humanity that might in their execution produce pregnancy, and I will remain steadfast in the assertion that violence rectifies not violence, horror banishes not horror, and that destroying the innocent brings not justice to the innocent, nor punishes the villain or rights the wrong.

You and I, dear reader, were never, nor will we ever be, something other or less than human from the moment we were conceived; for humanity and life has no beginning other than its beginning. We are not, nor were we ever, mere clumps of cells or parasites or extensions of the female anatomy until, at some indeterminate point, we became human beings. And we are no less human by our means of conception, whether through love or violence, or by our ability to live apart from modern medicine or machine—such would be a slippery slope for all, and inconsistent with the history of humanity, as many who live now by the advancements of the modern world perished in days past, and were mourned as lives lost.

We live because we have been divinely fashioned to do so;

our lives are owed not to the mercy of our mother for allowing us to survive our time in her womb to the moment we gasped our first breath and beheld our first light. There is no compromise with or conditional definition of life; and this piece, which gives a voice to the voiceless, aims to capture just that.

A blind culture has morphed the killing of the smallest and most helpless among us into something worth celebrating and shouting on the mountaintops; it has deadened the senses of the masses to the cries of our humanity and allowed us to look with indifference upon piled carcasses stuffed in drums; and it has coddled our ears, softened our hearts to the sting, and diverted the mind in its twisting of language, painting over the harsh and soul-spearing word ***infanticide*** with something cold, machine, and unfeeling.

I bear my teeth at the lie that has deceived many, not at the mother who contemplates or has had an abortion, regardless of her reason. My heart aches for every victim of this lie: the mothers, the fathers, the families and friends, and the children.

Who can fathom the depths of destruction forged by this abominable deception? Never in history has such a tremendous scope of unspeakable violence and injustice been perpetrated against mankind's most vulnerable and innocent of souls. Truly, who can fathom the depths of destruction forged by this abominable deception? And who can bear the price that must be paid?

This prologue and the story it precedes are not the culmination of my position; they are merely the articulation thereof. I compose thusly not to proclaim myself as righteous, nor to demonstrate myself as brave for speaking in contrast to, or for the sake of bucking, popular culture; bravery is a mother protecting the helpless innocent inside her, even in the midst of turmoil, even when the road ahead is uncertain or paved with vile injustice, even when the child bears the face of her abuser; bravery is demonstrated by she who places the life of another above her own, regardless of circumstance.

Though I have ever held this position and been an opponent of abortion, my belief in regard to the severity of that which I oppose and the views I have long held have in recent times been given greater depth and a much firmer, more fortified foundation. I believe all children are by God knit together in the womb of their mothers, and that all mothers have been by the same Creator knit; it is my commitment, therefore, to love and to serve all who are so divinely loved, that they might be lifted from whatever darkness points them toward this lauded evil and destructive lie, and bring forth another chance for the light of Heaven to shine forth to a dying world, rather than condemn it to the darkness.

Thank you, my dear reader, for reading and taking the time to consider the view of another. Such is, unfortunately, a rare trait in our world today.

What
will I
be?

What Will I Be?

What will I be?

When comes the light to call me home,
When meet I whom I long have known,
When there at last, what will I see?
What will I feel?
What will I be?

There is a greater warmth that lies
Beyond the cold that waits outside.
It calms the storms; it binds and keeps,
And shelters those who in it sleep.

What cruel vibrations did me wake;
How violently did my world quake.
And how it trembles even still.
Torment in tender heart o'erfills.

When from this world I cut the cord
And unto newness climb aboard
A ship of dreams, of wonders grand,
E'er with thee, walking hand-in-hand.

The noise has ceased, the screams, the wails;
Yet echoes in my world prevail.

They haunt this blood, a whisp'ring curse,
And urge my fate with statements terse.

What will I be? Perhaps like you?
Will e'er these lips speak what is true?
Might I ascend? Or will I fall?
With thee to guide me through it all
Peace will be mine, and ne'er I'll fret.
Thy love this heart will ne'er forget;
And with thee deep inside, you'll see
How I will fly,
What I will be.

O, falling rain—wilt thou ne'er cease?
How long until thy clouds know peace?
O, sun—why dost thou hide thy face?
And from this blessing joy erase?

What name for me hast thou prepared?
How might it sound when on the air
It floats so gently from thy lips,
And meets my cheek with tender kiss?

Such silence, now. 'Tis e'er so still.
Yet eerie tremors o'er me rill.
They trickle softly, slowly, deep,
And wake me to eternal sleep.

I long for thee, to be more near
To thee! And with each coming year

To know thee more and better still,
To be through thee wholly fulfilled!

From interim abode I'll fly
Into a world of endless sky,
Wherein at last I'll meet the one
Who'll hold me close
And call me son.
And if there is no more for me
Let me at least
Your dear son be.

The time has come! How soon the light
To call me forth from dawning night
Appears above my head. I go,
Too soon, I fear; too soon, I know.
Am I prepared? How will I stand
On legs so weak? And with these hands,
So small and new, how will I hold
Your outstretched palm, banishing cold?
But if your outstretched hand awaits,
Hasten me now to your embrace!
Take me gladly unto your love!
Look, there! My world opens above!
Your metal arms reach now for me!
O, what awaits!
What will I

Prologue: With All My Heart, Forever

JUST as the Christmas holiday festivities got underway here at the Route 27 Publishing® headquarters, a most interesting happening happened that I simply must share with you.

As I have mentioned, Conners is presently employed in the writing of his novels, which we hope to release soon; and for one series in particular, he and I (mostly I) have spent a great deal of time meeting with and interviewing the characters, doing all we can to ensure we capture as accurately as possible their stories and the overall grand tale. Doing so sometimes produces a sort of bond (something like friendship, I suppose), which, during the holidays, when so many souls are imbued with the Christmas spirit, leaves one at risk of being the recipient of a gift.

Don't get me wrong: I love gifts. However, I'm more the type who understands full well that I really don't need another *thing* taking up space in my house, but also sees others' homes and hearts as empty spaces in desperate need of material knick-knacks to fill the void.

Conners, on the other hand—while he, too, does enjoy a tame giving and receiving—tends to ponder and contemplate the implications, imputations, and ins and outs of the gifts he is given, until he has worked himself into so wild a mental hurricane that I have no choice (yet, all the pleasure in the world) to grab the emergency tranquilizer gun from the closet for some good ol' fashioned target practice.

Christmas is such a wonderful time, is it not?

Anyway, this Christmas, one of the characters in this three-part novel series gifted the Route 27 Publishing® staff a goat.

We each got a goat.

A living, breathing, and probably spitting goat.

Only, *we* didn't get the goat.

A goat was donated on our behalf to a family in need.

I was tickled pink at the idea—how incredibly thoughtful, thought I! Not to mention 'twas also a welcome relief for the limited space in my tight living quarters! And I had just sat down to compose a jolly "thank you" letter, when my employer walked slowly into the room, reading the card he'd received from the character, explaining the donation.

Author: "It's kind of a strange gift, isn't it?"

Narrator looks up from writing, sees Author standing in doorway, rubbing chin as one would a piece of fruit at a grocery store

Narrator: "What is? The goat? I think it's—"

Author: "Yes, yes; I thought it was strange, too. And for the life of me I can't tell which part is stranger: the goat, or the fact that it has been purchased in my name. I mean, some family I have never met will get a gift I never saw, for which I never paid, and to them never consciously gifted; and, should they have any manners—See? I don't even know them! They may have no manners at all!—they'll thank *me* for the goat! They'll gather 'round a glass of warm and chunky goat's milk, raise a barbequed goat's leg, and lift a cheer to Mr. C. K. Conners: the generous mystery man from far away! Or, if indeed they are devoid of manners—Gosh, how rude are these people, anyway?—they'll chug those milk chunks and scarf down carnivorous mouthfuls of goat meat without so much as a grateful nod in my general direction! They'll slap me upside the face with this most blatant rudeness, and I won't even have the satisfaction of knowing about it! Do you have any idea how humiliating it is to be slapped and also be the last to know? What's funnier still is that never in my life have I *wanted* a goat. Never! And now that I have been gifted a goat that has been given away for me, I kind of want a goat… more specifically, I want *that* goat. It's bad enough to get a gift you have no chance of keeping, but is instead pre-re-gifted—it's all the more cruel to be made to want the thing you had never wanted and never had until today, but have already had given away, whether you like it or not! Furthermore—"

Narrator: "Any further and we'll be miles away from where we started—much further, even, from the neighborhood of Sanity. Not sure if there's any going back from that kind of madness—*you're* proof of that."

Author: "Furthermore—says the man who pays your salary—and undeterred, I must now wrestle with the conundrum regarding whether theses feelings mean I am a heartless person."

Narrator quickly raises hand

Narrator: "I think I can solve that riddle for you!"

Author heaves a weary sigh as he folds Christmas card and slips it into top pocket

Author: "A Christmas headache: that's what he's given. Excuse me."

Author turns to leave; faces hall. Narrator swallows frustration at having been commanded to excuse (See Ramblings Part One, Page 30, beginning at final paragraph)

Narrator: "Where are you going?"

Author still facing hall

Author: "North. I'm sure some farmer or other has a goat for sale."

Narrator: "You're actually going to buy a goat?"

Author: "Yup. And I'm going to sacrifice it on our little gift-giver's doorstep."

Narrator ponders the perception of heroism the public might bestow if he took this chance to save the world from the madman Conners

Narrator: "You wouldn't."

Author: "No. But I won't let him have any of the milk."

Neither goats nor milk nor Christmas have anything to do with our next story, *With All My Heart, Forever.*

Our forthcoming, literary arrangement is a tale told through the eyes of several characters, each in his or her own time as the story progresses. How the narrative flows through much of the beginning is not made clear: Are these a series of reflections before we arrive in the present; is the story playing out in a linear fashion, the events happening one after the other; or, have we the record of something left behind, intercut with scenes from days past? I can tell you that Conners did approach the composing of this piece with one of these specifically in mind; however, he remained conscious of the fact that the considering of other possible perspectives could add something to the reading experience. Beware, of course, not to add or subtract any elements to fit the mold of a particular point of view, for every word was carefully and deliberately placed. Consider, only, how the possibilities can further reveal the message, rather than how they can be used to form new messages.

Now, what of inspiration?

On his drive home from visiting an old friend, a very popular song came over the radio. Familiar with the chorus, Conners took the opportunity presented by the long drive to listen intently to the lyrics—this he did without any expectation for what he might hear; it was merely curiosity that sparked this intent listening. And if the cat was the veil of a catchy tune and sing-along-able chorus, then, I can say with absolute certitude, that the cat was by curiosity most thoroughly killed.

It is no novel experience in the modern age to have the aura of a popular, catchy tune shattered by the investigating of its lyrics; one could even consider composers of old and find some shocking or unexpected themes, motivations, and even lyrics in otherwise heavenly-sounding musical arrangements. But this aura-shattering, despite the commonality of the phenomenon, proved most shocking. How opposite an analysis Conners would have given in supposition regarding this song's message had you asked him while he yet knew only the chorus; and how thoroughly razed was any regard he'd held for that song, now that the true meaning had been laid bare…as ever it had been before his deaf ears.

Almost immediately, as the lyrics sank beneath the surface, there played before him scene after scene in the story of a man: like in action to the one in the song was he, but not fully in character arc.

The scenes you are soon to read are true in their composition to those the Author imagined while he should have been eyeing the road; and when he had at last made it home, with only a shrubbery lodged in the grill of his car, a stop sign through the passenger side of the windshield, and a dazed jogger sprawled atop his roof, Conners sat right down and composed the tale.

It would indeed be injudicious to approach this story with the hopes of gleaning from the context which song specifically had ignited the spark of inspiration, and I have not identified the song here, because that element is irrelevant to and would serve only to distract from the point, as the song was merely a spark of inspiration, rather than a foundation—that song and this next piece tell not the same tale. Take the story for what it is; absorb the message it seeks to convey; and listen carefully.

Have at it.

With
all my
heart,
Forever

With All My Heart, Forever

I remember our wedding day.

IT was autumn; the sky was clear, the air was cool; and not a single color was in the grand display unrepresented—though, in my eyes there was but one color: white.

As she crossed the threshold and onto the grassy aisle—stepping out from beneath the white, ivy-laced, wooden archway that had kept her in patchy shadow—gliding to her father's arm, seeing her became a near impossibility. Such exquisite grace and loveliness rare is like the unobstructed sun that blessed our special day; and, coupled with the heart beating beneath that blossoming burst of unbridled beauty, that tender heart known well by my own, these eyes were helpless against the overwhelming tide of emotion that quickly swallowed them whole into glinting pools, warm and unquenchable.

How could a man ever be so fortunate as to have someone love him willingly, unconditionally, wholly; to have the one he loves requite his adoration and say "yes" to a proposition of lifelong companionship, partnership, trust, and devotion? How could a man ever hope to see in the eyes of his beloved that which burns in his own eyes, and know—*truly* know—that what he has found has found him, as well? And how could I, so unworthy a man, deserve even the casual acknowledgement of the one who moves now to take my hand in hers, becoming mine, as I will be hers, and she and I one?

These thoughts return unto me, are brought back to life, now, as I, after all these years, look again upon those two smiling faces from long ago.

I have cherished this photograph deep in my heart; though, it has been some time since I have looked upon it. In fact, I wonder if I have ever looked upon it since the day it arrived with the others. Surely, I must have seen it at least once more after that, but I cannot recall any such moment. What I do recall, however, and vividly, is the moment this photo had and has captured. I am taken back into the body of my youth, transported deep within my very soul to a moment that had upon it been imprinted, but had, until now, become buried by the burdens my existence has since bought and born.

I remember.

I remember her touch, her smile, and the love that was imbued within them and had these things brought into being.

I remember her words, her vows, and the fervency with which she'd made them.

I remember her life, and the life she had ignited in and given unto me.

I remember her.

I remember.

I remember.

***

"Morning."

"Is it morning already?"

"Sure is."

"Boy. What time is it?"

"Does it matter? We've got all day, haven't we?"

"If it was the weekend, maybe. But I've gotta get going—big meeting on the agenda."

"I can wait."

"You'll be waiting a while, remember? I've got a plane to catch! I really should have flown out yesterday, but—"

"But I'm just too persuasive."

"Well, yeah…I guess. Anyway, I need to catch that plane; the meeting is this evening."

"When will you be back?"

"Couple days."

"That long?"

"It's not *that* long!"

"I know. It's just—it's just, well, I feel like I don't ever get to see you anymore."

"Don't be dramatic! You see me! I've just got a lot of, you know, *other* things going on—you know that."

"Well, maybe if—"

"Meg, look, I'll be back in a couple of days. We can discuss this then. Right now I have to go. How's my tie?"

"A bit crooked; but, then again, you did just set a world record for dressing yourself."

"I'll see if my time qualifies for the summer Olympics. How about now?"

"Dashing."

"Great. Well, um…I'll, uh…I'll be seeing you."

"Wait!"

"*What*, Meg? I really have to go!"

"You forgot this. Wouldn't want to be seen without it, now

would you?"

"Goodbye, Meg."

***

She never let me down. Not once.

My job took me all over the country. Sometimes, I would be gone for a week or two, maybe more; but she would always be there waiting for me at the airport when I returned.

One is exposed to any number of relationships over the course of his or her lifetime, relationships they can observe, and from those observations draw conclusions and learn. And one of the many cynical conclusions I had drawn, that my bride definitively defied, was the befalling of an eventual and inexorable boredom, a complacency regarding one's partner.

I believed it was inevitable for the ecstasy of youth and the passion that leaves one drunk with love to prove fleeting. How often I had seen couples sitting in silence in restaurants, or acting independent of one another—acting as if the other didn't even exist, the way children do following what grownups might call a petty quarrel.

It was only a matter of time, I thought, before a pair began to feel more like they were tolerating one another, existing side by side, rather than actively loving and living as one.

These observations and conclusions from examples that had unto me been presented left me apprehensive to enter the marriage game. But—as is the tale for most—the Love Bug bit me before I could squash it underfoot; and I found myself in a position defiant of all I had deemed rational: kneeling, and kneeling before someone who I had convinced myself would quell my every reservation and prove my pessimistic views unfounded.

And she did.

Though it shouldn't have affected me thusly, I was, every time, surprised to see my bride's elated reaction to my emergence from the airport terminal following a business trip. Without fail, she would let out an excited little yelp, rush through the crowd, and jump into my arms, kissing me all over, as if I had just returned from a long tour of military duty, when I had actually been but sitting in stuffy conference rooms for the past few days. She held me every time as if for the last time, as if for the first time after an endless season of modest forbearance; as if for all time.

Why—maybe the word is "how"—was she always so excited? Who am I that she should wait for me, that she should want me?

Who am I?

Perhaps I should have asked those questions then, and more often.

With all that hung on my mind and body following a trip, it was difficult for me to break free of my desire to find a nice, quiet place on a couch in my own home, and there let my pores slowly detox from the mental and physical sicknesses of business travel.

I look back now and realize that I never fully appreciated those moments, as I should have. I was selfish—not what she deserved. And yet, her excited yelp never lost volume, her rush through the crowd never slowed, her leap never missed its mark, and her kisses never cooled.

I miss those moments.

I miss the sound of her yelp.

I miss seeing the staid businessmen and clueless tourists getting body-checked as she sprinted through the crowd.

I miss having to drop my briefcase and jacket to catch my flying bride.

And I do so miss her kisses.

I miss those moments.

I miss her.

I miss *her.*

***

"Have I ever told you how beautiful you are?"

"In words? I'm not sure. But I think I've gotten the message."

"You're beautiful, Meg."

"In what way?"

"What?"

"Do you mean *physically* beautiful?"

"Of course!"

"*Only* physically?"

"You know that's not what I meant! You proposed in query and for clarification one of the ways in which the word 'beautiful,' lifted in compliment, might have—by virtue of my intention for choosing said word—been defined; and I answered affirmatively, avowing that your proposed definition of the word 'beautiful' fell under the umbrella of commendation that my statement, describing you thusly, had intended to convey."

"You could have just said 'no.'"

"And given you the satisfaction of being in control—*never*!"

"Oh, you think this is about control, do you?"

"Absolutely! Why else would you ask a buckshot-loaded

question like that?"

"*Buckshot?*"

"Yeah! Had I answered in any way that could have been twisted into something I'd never intended, I might as well have been riddled to Swiss cheese!"

"Well, if you're the one in control of this conversation, why don't you make me see just what you meant by 'beautiful?' What exactly is under this umbrella of yours, good sir?"

"I think…I think you just snatched control away from me."

"You're no match for the likes of my chromosomal composition, buddy! Now, start spouting!"

"All right, all right. Well, let's see, um…you're, uh…"

"*Well?*"

"I…"

"What's the matter?"

"Nothing…nothing. I need to get going, anyway."

"Where are you going?"

"I'm meeting the guys tonight, remember?"

"Oh, right. Hey, are you okay?"

"Yeah, yeah. I'm fine."

"I'm not mad, you know—just joking."

"No, no; I know. I just need to go. I'll see you."

"Don't forget."

"What?"

"This."

"Oh, right. Darn it. Keep forgetting."

"I know."

"Well, I'll see you, Meg."

"Bye."

***

It's hard to be faced with what you cannot be.

We had tried for years, and nothing happened. We knew something was wrong. We'd somehow stumbled into a cliché, the kind one sees over and over on the silver screen, and, thus, feels is a mere fiction that affects only those who aren't you. It was no more real for me than it would have been for anyone privy to our story.

And yet it was real, and I was to blame.

There would be no chance for she and I to start a family of our own. After looking over other options, I began to wonder if she and I could have even afforded what we had been trying to conceive, because there was no way, then, that our means could have covered what alternatives were to us being presented.

I couldn't be a father, and I had failed as a provider: failed to meet one of my wife's deepest desires. Often I would steal a glance at her gazing longingly at her abdomen—sadly, with a deep wondering in her eyes; but she never said a word. She never shed a tear, none that I ever saw. She never looked at me in a pleading or disappointed manner. She never let me see how devastated I know she must have been.

And yet, I felt it.

The pain of my failure, I know, was not radiated from her and into me; it was sown and reaped within my very core, its seed falling over my fingertips. Facing her became increasingly difficult. I had to distance myself to forget, to keep my mind from exploding. It was easier, so much easier, to just be away.

And, so, I made myself scarce.

I had meant for it to be temporary, but I soon found it so comfortable to be on a plane, in a stuffy conference room, or someplace else, with my mind resting contentedly on something other than my bride sitting at home and wondering what might have been had I been something, or someone, other than who I was, who I am.

How gradually my inwardly aimed bitterness had tainted my vision, until I had created something I know, and knew then, was not real.

Temporary.

That's what it was supposed to have been.

I had foolishly believed that more work, more being away from home, would somehow help me get past my failures, my weaknesses, that I could forget via some harmless diversion and release.

Looking back, I see I had but wasted precious time and made myself all the weaker. And, looking back, I see all the more just how wonderful, how invaluable, and how unbelievably beautiful is my bride; for through it all she stood by my side.

She was loyal and true, devoted, attentive, and affectionate.

I was blind to it all.

It was easier to be away.

It was easier to be diverted.

It was easier to be relieved.

It was easier to be absent.

It was easier to be ignorant.

It was easier to run.

It was easy.

***

"Remember when we first met?"

"What about it?"

"I'm just asking if you remember. Do you recall that day?"

"Sure, I do."

"What do you remember?"

I remember being spread thin. I remember seeing a black sun, feeling a wintry breeze rushing through the summer scorch. I remember me, being trapped within my own head, having myself in the crosshairs, wrestling with myself, being locked in a death stare with my own eyes, seeing only what I was not, what I couldn't be, what I felt I should have had, what was from my perfect portrait lacking.

And then I saw…

To be released from one's own clutches in an instant is a violent experience, but the escape it brings, the relief it samples upon the tongue, makes one instantly drunk with its sweet nectar and enamored with, even enslaved by, its source. For me, that source was she: a rare vision, the likes of which these eyes, which had but gazed upon my wretched self all my life, believed they had never seen before—though, a small part of me was certain this was not true.

A sight for sore eyes?

No.

More like a sight for unveiled eyes, a sight for the ages, like looking into the sun—a sensation that, in the moment, felt familiar, just as sensations experienced when eyes are closed leave behind remnants of feeling that cause one to sense that what has ignited those remnants must be the stuff of dreams come to life.

But of the dream, whence scattered remnants left behind had been that day ignited, I could remember nothing.

My mind, like my eyes, could see only…

"Me?"

"I'm not talking to myself, here, am I? Yes, *you*! Do you need me to repeat my initial question?"

"Sure; of course—I mean, no! Um, well…you were there, and…"

"Boy, we're sure off to a good start, huh? C'mon! This will be fun! Tell me what you remember! What were you thinking?"

"I remember thinking…"

"Yes?"

"Well, I guess I didn't do much thinking. I was a bit overtaken, you might say."

"As was I."

"Oh, knock it off, Meg! I'm no prized pig, or anything."

"Prized pig? You sure you want to be called my prized pig?"

"You know what I meant!"

"Do I?"

"I meant I'm nothing special."

"You are to me."

"And *I*, in turn, question your judgment."

"I don't! You hooked me that day like no one else had ever been able to do."

"I doubt that."

"It's true! Don't you remember what you said to me?"

I remember.

Boldness like I had not felt in some time exploded within me, like a volcano; and into my veins flowed a thick, molten confidence that would, as I marched to her side, compel me to leave my life in a heap in my wake.

A master of one-liners I most certainly am not, but whatever opener I'd offered earned me a spot in the seat opposite hers; and with every bolt of the fiery lightning impacting me from the glitter in her eyes and smiles from her perfect lips, my inhibitions crumbled a little more to the wayside, until hours had passed and several iced coffees apiece had filled our bladders nearly to the bursting point and rendered our nerves like sparking power cables—at which point I said, "Yes."

Though, that word was not from my lips poured forth. It was conveyed in gesture, a powerful gesture.

"I said a lot of things that day."

"You sure did! You talked so fast and at such great length, I thought I'd never get to contribute to the conversation!"

"Well, I was nervous! I had also pounded like four coffees."

"And it was adorable."

"I'm glad you think so; but that 'adorable' performance, without a doubt, is responsible for some of these 'adorable' grey hairs."

"C'mon! You remember what you'd said, don't you? We wouldn't be here right now if you hadn't have said it."

The gravity of my words that day still makes me weak in the knees.

What I said was nothing more than a cliché—it was nothing special in composition, nothing original. People have for ages said to persons of interest exactly what I said that day; but I wonder if any of those speakers ever said those words in so consequential a manner as I had done. Truly, those seven, simple words changed my life completely and forever.

After hours of outpouring, connecting with a complete stranger, as if she and I had known each other since childhood, and feeling as if the stars had realigned themselves in my universe and were singing in harmony a song of blessed destiny, I, emboldened as ever, laid my hand gently atop hers and said, "Where have you been all my life?"

"Exactly!"

"Really? That's the part you remember most?"

"Of course! Because I was thinking the exact same thing! It was like it was meant to be!"

"Yeah."

"Oh, you and your sham aversion to romance! I *know* you—deep down you're a romantic! A real Romeo!"

"Romeo, eh?"

"Yes! '*Wherefore art thou Romeo?*'"

"*Wherefore art thou Romeo?*"

Why, indeed.

Why did you have to be a Romeo? Why a Romeo, and not a Benedick? Or a Darcy? Or a Bob-darned-Cratchit!

Why couldn't you have been better?

Why couldn't…no.

Why *didn't* you?

"Well, Juliet, I've gotta run."

"But it's only midnight!"

"And my flight leaves at 2 A.M."

"Can't you stay just a half-hour longer? Please? It's been so long since—"

"I know it has; but I've been, you know…really busy lately."

"Just five more minutes?"

"I'm sorry. I have to go. Where's my tie?"

"Here."

"Thanks. Well, I'm off. Bye, Meg."

"Wait! You forgot your—"

***

This photograph, how adored it is in my heart: she holding my hand, I holding hers; united as one.

As I gaze into these eyes frozen in time, I can feel the pulsing of her heart running through my fingers, just as it had done on the day this photo was taken.

How could a man have ever been so fortunate?

Look at me.

This man?

This man?

Why me?

Darn it, why *me*!

Didn't she know she could have done so much better than *me*? Look at my pathetic face! How dare that face be framed beside hers—how *dare* that face! And what is in that little head? That tiny, worthless head fitted so out of place next to this angel! Did that hideous face and the third-rate fool behind it have any idea how fortunate he was? Could that worm of a man comprehend how good a lady to whose arm he had affixed his deplorable existence? Did he really know then how out-of-this-world-lucky he was? Were those rosy thoughts really swirling about his head, or was he instead absorbed in himself? Did he really recognize the depths of his unworthiness, or were his thoughts otherwise occupied, dwelling on all the fun and pleasure his bride could bring him in the coming years?

I remember our wedding day…the way *he* had seen it.

It was autumn; the sky was clear following the rain that had made the earth a giant pigsty the night prior for our outdoor wedding, making my life a mess of complaints from guests about ruined shoes and whatnot; the air was freezing; and all I could think about was how much more it was going to cost me to return the rental chairs and tables and other assorted pieces of overpriced garbage that had been ruined by the mud—not to mention my own shoes and tux.

As she crossed the threshold and into the muddy isle, stepping out from beneath that costly wooden archway that had kept her in patchy shadow, to take her father's arm, I could think of nothing other than how much I despised that old man. Sunglasses would have been a beneficial touch; my eyes were nearly weeping from the direct barrage of sunlight.

Did I ever stop to consider or recall the fact that she'd asked for none of this, that it had been not her voice demanding extravagance? Did I ever take a step back to ponder how a man could ever be so fortunate as to have one so rare give her love to him? Did I ever wonder how I, so unworthy a man, could ever have been granted even the casual acknowledgement of the angel who moved that day to take my hand in eternal union?

No.

These thoughts are born in me, are brought to life, *now*, as I, after all these years, look again upon those two smiling faces from long ago.

I cherish this photograph deep in my heart—oh, how I wish I had looked upon it sooner! Would it have helped? I'd like to think it would have.

As I gaze into the eyes of my bride, I am stricken with a wave of cold, as in my mind forms a chilling question:

Did I ever love her?

Did I?

I do now.

***

"What are you doing?"

"Huh?"

"Sorry! Didn't mean to startle you. I asked what you were doing."

"Oh! Oh, um…nothing. Just, um, you know, just organizing…organizing a few things."

"Looks like you're packing. Are you going somewhere?"

"Uh, yeah, yeah; I am."

"Another business trip?"

"Something like that, yeah."

"Kind of short notice, huh?"

"I guess so."

"Another one of those three-day deals?"

"Mmm."

"That's not so bad. Bringing your backpack this time, I see."

"What? Oh. Yeah."

"What's that you're taking with you?"

"Nothing, really. Nothing."

"Can't be nothing—let me see!"

"It's nothing! Don't—"

"*Oh*! It's our wedding picture!"

"Yeah. Yeah, our wedding picture."

"I love this one. I think it's my favorite. You look so handsome!"

"…So do you—er, um, beautiful, that is."

"Why are you taking it like this? I could put it in a frame for you, so it won't get damaged."

"No, no. That's okay. We can just leave it here."

"No! I want you to take it with you! I hate it when we're not together during these trips—this way I can be with you!"

"Sure. Fine. That's okay, I mean. You can put it in a frame."

"Great! Oh, honey, what's this? Did you lose your ring?"

"What?"

"Your wedding band."

"Oh…oh, darn it. I must have forgot—lost it; I must have lost it someplace."

"I'm sure it's here somewhere. I'll look for it while you're gone."

"…Thanks."

"Okay! I'll get this in a frame for you. Be right back!"

***

When I returned to the office, he was gone.

The front door was open, his truck was not in the driveway,

and his backpack was resting on his desk, its contents spewing forth from its mouth, just as they had been when I had startled him minutes before, causing him to upset it.

I had heard his truck revving and driving away, but I had dismissed it as being the merely neighbor's car—my husband was waiting for me in his office; he wasn't leaving just yet. Last minute trips are a normal thing for him, I know; but he's never been so abrupt as not to give me a farewell kiss.

He couldn't have left for his trip, not with his briefcase and backpack still here.

I wonder where he went.

Seeing him gazing with misty eyes at our wedding photograph was a pleasant surprise today.

I have been so worried about him as of late.

He's been distancing himself from me.

I know he has been.

Just the other day I walked into his office to offer him some coffee—he yelped as if a bomb had gone off, then just stared at me with incredibly wide eyes for a really long time.

He's eating himself from within, that's what's happening; that's what's been causing all this odd behavior. I've tried everything to make him understand that his inability to give us children does not change the fact that I love him with all my heart. But I know my husband better than anyone, and I know how hard he is on himself. If he believes or convinces himself that he cannot be useful, he feels worthless; and his definition of useful is a bar set so high, no human could ever reach it.

I have never been able to understand why he cannot see the value he brings, the value within him. Often has he asked me, with all sincerity, why I had agreed to marry him. That's easy:

I love him; I want to be his partner, his lover, his servant, his friend—I want to support him in any way I can; to comfort him, help him, and be whatever he needs me to be.

This may be what my decision has *become*—Heaven knows I am not the woman I was.

Regardless of where we'd started, he and I can still set upon the right path. The jarring of our bumpy road, his and mine, thew my feet onto a new way. If he wants to, we can walk this way together; with my entire being I pray we will.

I'm still beside him, clinging tightly to his hand—how I hope he looks this way before the paths diverge.

Much work has yet to be done.

But it's not a labor.

It's a marriage.

What's this?

His backpack doesn't have any business related things in it.

There's nothing in it, actually, save for this envelope.

It's already stamped, but not sealed.

It's addressed, too.

Who's…

Who's Meg?

***

"What is it?"

"Dunno. Lotta commotion over there, though."

"Sure is. Boy, I hope nobody's hurt."

"I heard something about an accident."

"Back *there*? Like a car accident?"

"Guess so."

"In a forest preserve parking lot? How reckless could somebody have been in a forest preserve parking lot that would warrant all this hoopla?"

"Maybe they were drunk?"

"Well, I suppose if—hey, ask *him*!"

"Officer! Excuse me, officer!"

"Back up, please, gentlemen. This area is being sealed off."

"What happened?"

"Darned shame. A young man was found dead."

"No!"

"Yeah. Darned shame. We found him in the woods, a little ways off the path. Got a call from a trail jogger; said they'd heard a gunshot."

"Murder?"

"Not sure yet. A darned shame."

"Who is he?"

"Couldn't say even if I knew—you understand. Said too much already, anyway. Now, if you'd please, gentlemen, we've got to get this area sealed off. C'mon, now. Let's go."

***

Two days had passed before any word of my husband was returned to me.

When he didn't come back the night I last saw him, I called

the police. His car, along with all his identification, was found the next morning parked outside the local grocery store; he was still missing.

Early that afternoon, I returned to his office to look for any clues as to where he might have gone. I had stuffed the letter to Meg in his backpack and then completely forgot about it—though, I wonder if it would have reentered my mind eventually had I not discovered one of his sealed drawers unlocked and an empty box of pistol ammunition lying therein.

After immediately informing the police of my findings, I began calling every number in the phonebook; I even called local businesses and any other number I could find to ask if anyone had seen my husband.

No one had.

I didn't sleep at all that night.

How could I have done?

Oh, dear heavens!

Where is my husband?

At exactly three minutes past seven this morning, I received a visit from the chief of police.

He didn't have to say a word.

I spent the rest of the day in confusion.

Why?

No other words came to mind.

Just, *why*?

I took no calls, answered no doors, and let not one shred of light pass through any window.

Tirelessly, desperately, I played out in my mind every

conceivable scenario until the moon had faded and the eastern horizon was set ablaze somewhere beyond my fortress of darkness.

And then…a thought entered into my head.

That envelope.

Maybe this Meg knew something I did not.

Maybe he had confided in her something he felt he could not confide in me, something that would help me piece together this horrible puzzle, and in so doing discover an answer.

I raced to my husband's office, snatched the letter from his backpack, switched on his desk light, an unfolded the contents of the unsealed envelope.

My hands trembled and my jaw chattered as I laid flat a hand-written letter—my husband's notoriously sloppy hand—and began to read.

Meg,

I can no longer live with what I have done. It was wrong of me to allow myself to become involved, and I must put an end to it before it's too late.

The consequences of our relationship are mine to bear. Whatever you and I might have felt for one another is irrelevant; for I had, before our meeting at the coffee shop, already pledged myself wholly to another. I have dishonored both you and my wife. For that, and more, I am truly sorry.

You said to me, once, that you knew for sure I loved you and not my wife, for no man who loves a woman could be unfaithful to her—you even joked that my neglect for my wedding band was proof of your assertion. I wish I could say you were wrong. Regardless, I must now make this right. What I made with you—and what I in turn did to my wife—was wrong; and nothing can change that, or remedy the damage it has caused.

You needn't forgive me—just forget me.

Goodbye.

***

The rest of the day was spent in silent reflection. What else might I have done?

What did I feel?

I felt what I feel now; though, I don't think I can describe it well enough that it might be understood. I feel weightless, I guess. I'm hollow. I'm weak. My blood is thin; my skin tingles. The tips of my fingers are like ice, but my neck and cheeks burn with painful fire. The rest of me is numb and somewhere between terribly restless and eerily relaxed. Often I feel a surge of ambition to rise from the chair to which I have been attached for who knows how long, to rise and take some sort of action: eat, perhaps; throw something, break something, put a hole in a wall; lie down and sleep, drift into the void of my whirling, tormenting thoughts; scream at the top of my lungs; pace aimlessly about the dark, empty house; cry until I wither and die. But those jolts grow weaker and weaker; they weren't very potent at the onset, and not one since the first has succeeded in lifting so much as a finger, wiggling a toe, or causing my stagnant eyes to blink or divert from the patch of painted drywall into which they have burned a considerable hole since that letter fell from a limp hand to its present place upon the floor: right there, sitting face up, staring at me, though I cannot see it; making me sense its presence, though I can do nothing to remove it.

Some women in my position might spend this time I have wasted asking themselves "*why*?"

I spent enough time doing that long before reading the letter.

No answer came then.

I'll have no answer now.

Regardless, it really doesn't matter why.

Not now, and possibly not even then—or ever, for that matter.

Who cares why?

Who cares?

I can't.

I won't.

Because, regardless of the answer, whatever it might be, or might have been, I am left with no chance to—

Good heavens!

My peripherals just spotted a silhouette growing in the veiled window, approaching the door.

Could it be him? Please! Could it—

The shadow stuffs some stuff into the mailbox, and then promptly departs.

Just the mailman.

The mailman?

Is it morning already?

I've been sitting here for far too long.

Before it fades completely, maybe I can tap into some of the adrenaline from the jolt of seeing a ghost in the window, and so animate these legs to stand.

I may still have to roll myself off of it.

Won't know until I try.

One.

Two.

Three!

All right.

Now, let's see if some bills can divert the mind for a few minutes. Anything, I'm sure, will be better than the last however long it's been.

Junk mail.

Junk mail.

Junk mail.

Junk mail.

And…what's this?

A letter…

From my husband…

Sent from and to this house…

Addressed to me.

Where's my chair? The weakness is returning—these legs will soon crumble; these hands are frantic, shaking.

I have no reservations.

Whatever this is, I'm reading it.

My Dearest Bride,

Your reading this letter makes real a most absorbing fear, with which I have been wrestling ever since the man I have for so long buried deep within became the man I must regard each and every day in the mirror. I want so much to intercept this message and tell you in person, face to face, all I must from my chest release. Heaven help me; I don't know if I can.

Yesterday, while rooting through some forgotten desk drawers, I found a photograph of you and me on the day of our wedding. Since then my eyes have scarce looked upon anything else, save for you, when you came into the office to ask if I wanted any coffee. Though I had succeeded in concealing the object of my present preoccupation, not even a pair of lunar satellites could have eclipsed my stare. I know you'd noticed.

You looked to me, yesterday, exactly as you did on the day of our wedding; and I realized—in the moment that had bred my stare—that you have ever been so lovely, that you have but grown in beauty, that yours is a beauty forged deep within, which has given your entire being a light that has ever sought to penetrate the tomb of stone, lined internally with mirror glass, I had long ago erected about my selfish soul.

You and I, all those years ago, stood upon an altar of union, before a congregation of love and support; and to you I made a promise:

I pledged my heart wholly to you. But I never knew until today what it meant to do so, to love you; and I fear, even after all these years, that I have never bestowed upon you that which my selfish eyes could never see you lavishing upon me every single day. I wish I could beg for your forgiveness. I wish I could find a way to make good on my promise, to offer this heart, as I claimed then to have done, wholly unto you—please tell me that heart has not been irreparably sundered.

I want so desperately to change, to be a better man, to erase all the damage I have done, the pain I have caused. If I could but efface my existence up to this moment and start anew with you. . . I fear nothing could ever make amends. I'm so sorry. I don't think I can face this. I'm a coward. I'm so sorry.

Your love has changed me. It has brought me back, if only at the very end. Know, my dearest bride, that I am sorry, that I justify not my faults, and that I will be your burden to bear no longer. What this heart has left to pay in retribution and atonement is not and will never be enough to afford that which you have given freely and without fail—though, I do so wish it could be. I do love you—know this, my dearest: I do love you, if only now and with all my heart; and ever will I love you with an undying love.

Forever, my bride. With all my heart, Forever.

***

I awoke this morning with my husband's letter fresh in my mind, as if I had just moments ago read it for the hundredth time.

Never would I have suspected these things of my husband—they're just too awful. But now the ugly realities of the world have been made real to me; they can no longer be avoided. My eyes have at last emerged from the sheltered corner of the world to which they had withdrawn—so long ago, I can't remember when. They have looked intently upon that which they sought ever to ignore, that which makes not the fairy tale journeys we desire, but more importantly that which reminds us that everyone in this world is vulnerable, is weak, and will—though we may try so hard not to do so; though our weakness and vulnerability are no excuse for it—eventually, and possibly irreparably, fall.

Irreparable.

That word…can there be an irreparable fall?

Scars are inevitable; yet, scars are but reminders of afflictions and offenses that have healed. Are there wounds that simply *cannot* heal, or is it the wounded who halts the healing? Does the pain bring us some sort of paradoxical comfort? Do we become addicted to the pain? Or do we, the wounded, fear the scar would be not enough to remind us, or our offenders, of the severity that wound represents? Must we ever carve the knife, dig the nail, tear the flesh, so that the wound remains open, exposed to the passing time, where it might become infected, and in turn ravish the healthy flesh surrounding it; thus, making this single wound our defining affliction and mark?

Maybe.

Many times I have picked at my own scabs, unwilling to let or help them heal; and while I can speak not for anyone but myself, one whose plight measures not at all against the plight of most, I do believe that in the pain there is healing; I do believe that while the scars will ever remain, one can be made whole again.

And now I must ask myself this question:

Could I?

The warmth of the morning coffee is more appreciated today than I can ever remember it being. It provides a much needed soothing; though, I fear nothing will quite set my nerves wholly to rest.

Is any of this real?

My mind is flooded with these vivid, devastating images; they seem to swirl about in a collage, all flashing bright, blinding colors that each seek out and, like the snap of a viper, touch a specific emotion inside of me, rendering my body and mind a shaken mess. It's so much like a dream, all of this. I wonder if it had all been merely an eruption of all the fears I have so long suppressed; an eruption that burst forth from my heart and into my sleeping mind, filling my slumbering eyes with awful visions, torturous manifestations of my anxiety, my overwhelming dread for what may be, leaving me now to deal with the cooling lava, the memories of the horrid production my fears played for me in the night. Words hidden within my heart warn of this slavery to Fear; but so powerful is his rod, even enough to make me afraid to attempt an escape from under it.

Or, maybe, I'm asleep now.

Maybe *this* is my dream.

Here, with my steaming coffee, with the sound of birds singing merrily in the cool, morning breeze, I have peace; or, at least, the capacity to find it…rather, I have the capacity to surrender myself into it, to let go, to fall upon strength greater than my own. My recent past, in slumber or in waking, found me helpless, both by my hand and hands beyond my control—perhaps just one or the other; I'm not quite sure. Here, though I can do little to command the hands of others, I have my hands. And from my power I at last release them.

They're not idle anymore.

The warming of this coffee mug has been like clinging to an icicle. Lifted high in the stillness, the silent power that surrounds me, they feel as though they have finally come alive.

Maybe, now, I'm asleep.

Sleeping or not, my hands are awake.

My heart is ready.

***

Rays of golden sun sting my eyes as I shuffle about this empty space. Upstairs sits an empty bed, the sheets on one side tousled; undisturbed on the other.

On the calendar in the kitchen are marked the days of loneliness, when obligations away from home leave this house rather empty. Three days ago, I marked the calendar again; this time it was unexpected. There had been no mark on the calendar the morning I last saw him, nor did I anticipate it would receive such a mark.

But receive a mark it did, and it was my understanding that I would be from that day until tonight alone. That's how these quick, short notice trips have gone since the beginning: he leaves one day, does his business over the course of the next two, and arrives home the day following.

Why should this trip have been any different?

He'd told me this was another of the same.

As marked, this will be the order of things.

It will be, just like always.

And, like always, I have all day to prepare; so, I do.

He's coming home today.

I have to be ready.

He's coming home.

I have to look my best.

He's coming home.

I simply *have* to look my best.

He is coming home.

I know it.

He *is* coming home.

Night quickly arrives.

I always meet him at the airport; so, that's where I must go. Yes, the airport is always where I last see him before his absence begins, and this time I had not the chance to see him off.

But I have never *not* met him at the airport upon his return; so, that's where I'm going.

He has not called, but I can't remember a time when he ever did so.

Call or not, there has *never* been a business trip from which he hasn't come home.

And he left for a three-day business trip three days ago—that means he's coming home tonight.

He's coming home.

As I drive along through the night, the streetlights shining like the diamond he always wanted to buy me, the one I never wanted, the one he had intended to replace the ring he'd made out of rolled masking tape, on which he had inscribed with a blue pen our initials, the one I still have and am wearing right now, beaming with the same light that burned within me the day he gave it to me, when I'd watched the door through which he'd departed that night, as if life could not begin again until he once more passed through it; as I sit here, as dolled up as I can possibly be, hoping this might recall for him the days when I was younger, when he and I were so different, when I would with furious, gleeful excitement watch the closed door of my parents' house like I did the night of our first date, back when he and I were all and everything; as I stand here at the gate, waiting, like I did the day he met with my father to ask for my hand, the day I remember staring at a closed office door for what felt like a month, hoping good news would emerge from a conference featuring two parties who were not the best of friends; as I stand here, alive with anticipation, as I was on my wedding day, waiting behind a closed door before being presented to the man to whom I had already given my heart, wholly and forever; as I stand here, my palms sweating, just as they did in the waiting room, gazing at the closed door and hoping to Heaven the problem lay with me and not with him; as I stand here, biting my lip, hard, as I've done increasingly so since he established his habit of returning to me after long nights when I was not needed, smelling of drink and pleasure, the kind not found under this roof, nor in our bed; as I stand here, today, waiting anxiously, as I have done a thousand times before, all that has happened is allowed to play about my eyes, and I am again confronted with that question:

Could I?

I stare at the gate.
    Could I?
The world around me whizzes by, obliviously.
        Could I?
Waiting for him to round that turn.
            Could I?
He will.
                Could I?
He's coming home.
                    Could I?

Could I…forgive him?

With all my heart, Forever…

Prologue: Letter

THIS story is not about a letter—an *alphabet* letter, I mean. While I'm sure the Author (should he ever take the time to do so) could produce a definitive favorite alphabetical character from among the list, I doubt he'd ever boast such affection for it as to compose an entire piece in its honor.

Now, in the Introduction, I'd mentioned that these prologues are intended to give a bit of backstory on the forthcoming tale, and that you, dear reader, could take them as you please: before reading, after reading, or as kindling for your fire. In setting up this next piece, I will be defining two references made therein that some test readers deemed obscure; so, if you'd like to experience the tale as a bowling ball barreling down a bumper-less alley, give that finger a lick and the page a flick. Otherwise, if obscure references are to you like a mental gutter ball, just sit tight.

Penned on a rainy afternoon in May, this most recently composed of this sequel's seven was born out of a single line inspired by a national day of remembrance. This line was the spark igniting a two-hour, undisturbed writing session, in which was crafted the tale of a young woman and her hope of receiving a letter.

It seemed natural to Conners that the story should be told in reverse—a structure similar to, though not influenced by, a popular modern film. Composing thusly, Conners hoped to capture the essence of one walking through their own memory, as on a linear path—like a car shifting into reverse and driving back along the highway of life, taking in every sight and sound of note it had passed along the way, from last to first—until eventually coming to the place upon which the desperate emotion of the first scene rests, whence is begotten the very heart of all that has just been read.

As for the latter mentioned references, the focal character at one point grabs her Oxfords, which is a type of shoe; and the first line about a "boy on his bicycle" comes from a term sometimes used in the 1940s to refer to Western Union delivery boys.

Gosh, this was a quick one, huh? Just under 500 words. Consider this my gift to you, dear reader.

Forward!

Letter

Letter

JUST a boy on his bicycle, speeding down a dirt road. She saw him from a distance: a cloud of dust manifesting slowly into human form. It had been quite a while; though, she could not tell just how long. And in all that time, she had daily, hourly, pulled down the half-moon door to reveal only emptiness. Sitting barefooted on the front stoop in the early morning glow, she watched the boy stop at this house and that one, before pushing the pedals and kicking up dirt. Her heart pounded faster, harder with each passing second. Crossing over the road, the boy glided diagonally to the house beside hers, where he made hasty work of the task at hand; and then, reaching again into his bag, he looked up. As his eyes fell into hers, a pair of hearts came to a halt. With a kick against the dirt road, the boy, unable to detach his gaze, and biting softly his bottom lip, rolled slowly forward.

***

It was day one, just day one—stupid to expect something on the first day. Yet, though thusly she'd reasoned, as her hand pulled down the half-moon door and her eyes darted frantically about the emptiness, she had hoped this impossible chance would beat the odds; for in her heart she held a similar hope, one for a different sort of arrival, which would survive only if that for which she searched today would come to her door...and soon.

***

She wasted no time—no, not one second. Never had there been such swift folding, stuffing, licking, sealing, stamping, and addressing; though, the writing of the contents had been careful, deliberate, and slow. Snatching her black Oxfords, she bolted from the house, leaving mother with a farewell and notice of intended destination that sailed off her tongue quicker than her folding, and then sprinted down the dirt road faster than her sealing. She ran barefooted, envelope in one hand and Oxfords in the other. Haste was the key, and shoes would only slow her down; she could worry about being ladylike on the return trip. Skating across the floor, her dusty, dirty feet struggled to find traction; but the train had not yet left the station, nor had the carrier even arrived with his bag. There she waited on the platform, toes dancing and fingers twiddling, looking this way and that, wondering how she might phrase a request to the conductor to guard and deliver for her this precious cargo, should the carrier never arrive. Alas, he did so; and, taking with a smile and a shaking of the head at that which had been abruptly stuffed into his hand, even before a salutation had breached his lips, he mumbled something about youngsters, and then promised that, as far as he could manage, delivery would be just as swift as her speech when she'd recited for him a list of best carrying practices—enough words to fill ten of his bags, spoken in a single breath. The train arrived, the bag was loaded, and her specially signed and sealed cargo was tucked carefully into the carrier's breast pocket. Patting the dust from her dress, she watched until the train was out of sight, and then walked back down the waking, dirt road—black Oxfords beating against the glow of the sunrise—wondering all the while if, perhaps, there'd be something waiting for her at home.

***

Moving in again with mother seemed, on its face, a practical and enjoyable idea—a necessity, rather; though, she realized very quickly just how much she'd changed since moving into the city apartment, and how much time those changes demanded if she were to transition back into a younger way of living. Mother was a blessing; she had a way of softening father's natural bluntness, which was so very difficult to absorb during this time, and not quite as charming as she'd remembered. Still, it had been father who'd insisted on cutting into his weekly pay, the little it was, to buy what he called the sturdiest paper and the most permanent ink—wouldn't want whatever cruel elements were sure to befall to destroy this vital connection to hope. And, so, with the best paper in town, the finest ink pen, and a spritz of precious perfume dashed upon the writing canvas, she sat at the desk by the light of the mid afternoon, leaving all evening and all night to compose before the Monday morning train arrived to carry away the weekend post.

***

Emotions were high on that day; though, as she pondered its every moment, she was sure the film, when developed, would depict none of it—such was her hope, anyway. When the photograph is lifted from the envelope, wherever it might be, nothing less than model happiness and better days on which to reflect should meet the eyes: smiles, elegant dress, handsome face, perfect hair—at least, as far as the darned wind had allowed. One shot of the two of them, along with one of just her to be pinned or carried, however he chooses: these, when they arrive, will be wrapped in perfumed paper, marked with her hand. One of him stays with her.

***

Knees buried in the dirt, face drenched, mouth gaping, though unable to make a sound, she would not release the leg of his pants. One foot had already disappeared into the car—by Heaven and all her might, the other would go no further. Though she'd tugged and resisted, the strength of the hands seizing her, and the power of his duty, ripped her away and hurled her into the dirt, as he was sealed permanently into the car and carried into the distance, disappearing into a cloud of dust and smoke, while she, voice now liberated, screamed until a black nothingness overtook her. At least, that's what she'd felt in her heart the moment their embrace was released and he whispered his final goodbye.

***

He was supposed to have had more time. Moving her back into her parent's house in a single day seemed just plain crazy. Thankfully, the combined wages of a file clerk and a stenographer afford only modest living; there wasn't much to move. Returning to the country had been an attractive idea shortly after becoming immersed in the bustling city culture. Who knew the flashing lights that had filled her youthful eyes would so quickly fade in brilliance? Even he had mentioned wishing he could return to the sawmill. What little he did earn brought home enough food for the day, and her contribution kept patches on the old clothes, and, sometimes, bought a handful of berries from the market. The dream of returning to simplicity was strong, and often they talked about how it might be done—sometimes inventing mountains of impossibilities, just to share a laugh and a sigh. And then it happened. Though she would be leaving her shorthand for the free and elegant longhand she much preferred, she knew not one stroke of her pencil would ease her mind. Though he would be trading the office for the fields, they would be not the fields he'd known. And though they were disentangling themselves from the city, they would not do so together; and a return to simplicity would come to feel as likely as avoiding the thing about which she refused to speak a word.

***

During the blur of months he spent away, she had the opportunity to attend the cinema, where she watched a reel detailing the type of preparatory work most likely occupying his present. The whole show filled her with pride and confidence; she even allowed herself to feel a tad reassured, for the things she saw these strange men doing on the screen would be more than simple for the man she knew well—indeed, a veteran of the sawmill could perform this work in his sleep. No man was more fit for the task ahead than he, as far as she was concerned. But this feeling lasted only until the newsreel that followed. She left that day shaken, trembling to her bones. Over there, one's strength seemed to matter little. How many mighty had already fallen.

***

He'd been right. It had been only a matter of time. Unlike many, he had stayed back from joining right away, using the time before his number was inevitably called to prepare her for his absence. She wouldn't have stood in his way had he immediately left at the call to action, regardless of how desperately she would have wanted to do so. What she, and many like her, feared had now become a reality. And the day his notice came, she kissed him and filled him with the strength she knew he would need in the months to come, then closed the door and sobbed bitterly into her pillow.

***

They were called into a neighbor's apartment. Gathering with folks from every floor, they listened intently to the radio. An evening entertainment scare program of sorts, surely mistaken for a news report, filled the room with utter silence. Whatever this program was, she didn't like it one bit; it was too close to home, too timely, too realistic; and as it played, droning painfully in the ears and contorting the surrounding faces, she fought to convince herself that this was not real. The next morning, there seemed to be no topic more captivating than last night's program. Even the newspapers were shouting about it. This was real. There was no escaping it. And life was again about to change, and all too suddenly.

***

The closing of the sawmill had been devastating. Newly married, just getting started, they had, like everyone else, found themselves suddenly in a vehicle of life stripped of its wheels. Life had become survival, and many times even that seemed impossible. Taking the nothing they had, a path was set for a foreign world, where, by Heaven's blessing, they found hard work and a place to keep sleeping eyes dry, at least from rain. What little was theirs was everything and nothing; they knew well how quickly material crumbles into dust. His hand in hers, hers in his, and a hand to the sky—they needed no more than this.

***

Burying her head into his chest, as the sun did set in brilliant color behind the distant, rolling hills, she heaved a sigh of pure contentment, of rapturous love; and when his arms wrapped around her, she knew that, here, she was safe, at last and forever. Life had just begun; a bright and beautiful future lay ahead. While the world was caught up in its fast-paced revelry and jubilant, carefree chaos, there was no excitement or wealth that could tempt either from the eternity that rested in the other's arms. Together, they would face the adventure upon which they had, that very morning, embarked, and see it through, come what may. Theirs would be a most beautiful story. She knew it would be. And the story was just beginning.

Prologue: On the Wall

CONNERS is a killer: good days, lively atmospheres, hope for humanity—he's killed them all. But he is no more deadly than in one, single arena, an arena in which he has been the undisputed king, the indubitable sovereign, the peak potentate of this brand of butchery; and this crown he has held firmly atop his head since childhood.

This is his story…in a way.

Dear reader, what lies ahead is something for which it may be difficult to prepare you, for even modern scientific consensus agrees not with the most impressive demonstration of havoc wreaked to which I have been a witness. What's even more incredible is the duality of the moment here presented when all perspectives are considered. On the one hand, you have peace and comforting relief; and on the other side of that hand you have unbounded terror and unspeakable horror. After reading this tale, you may find yourself forever conflicted.

While some children were demonstrating their skill and aptitude in athleticism, arts and crafts, science, and mathematics, Conners was combining and exercising the lot with unconscious effort, honing himself into the stone-cold courier of Death he is today—with calm, cunning calculation he assesses the situation and his prey; employing his every sense and knowledge of his quarry's mind, down to its molecular foundation, he sets himself within the very exoskeletal body of the doomed, hypothesizing with expert accuracy its every thought and erratic movement; he forges a series of lures and traps, then glides through each with balletic grace, sweeping through the air like a wing-footed gazelle; and with a greater feat of speed and deadly accuracy than even the greatest gunslinger of old, he brings about a swift and chilling conclusion.

There is nowhere to hide…

…nowhere to run…

…and there is no escape.

Herein lies an interlude of sorts, should one be quick enough to spot it; and it is this forthcoming account that has puzzled the invented minds of those whose existences lie within a world of Conners' creation.

Amid the confusion and seemingly disoriented direction is a microscopic glimpse, magnifying the greater world in which we turn—not to mention we get a bit of insight into the minds of those we disregard or despise without ever getting to know them.

I'm not saying there is here anything profound to be found, nor am I saying this tale *lacks* any profundity; rather, this is a reexamination of something seen that needs to be seen once more. Still, I'm sure B.R.A.G. (the rather bumptious Bug Rights Activism Group) will draw from this story some other takeaway, fit to be morphed into a soapbox.

By now, I trust you've gathered from both the title and this little preamble ramble the entomological identity of our focal characters, as well as the part inspired by my employer. There's only so much I'm willing to do before it feels like I'm conducting my professional affairs as would my dream math teacher—that is, spoon-feeding the answers.

Prepare yourself, dear reader, to magnify your world through the microscope, as you follow our protagonists, Zurmenz and Grezzy, on their journey to explore, dissect, and define a realm beyond their own, while ever there looms about them the mystery and intrigue of one whose name is known well in tales of chilling fantasy and cemented in the pages of far-fetched legend: the one and only Bloomdale Assassin.

All that he becomes, this Bloomdale Assassin, when is caught the scent of intrusion and is glimpsed the streak of annoyance, defies that which the world thinks it knows, what laws it thinks it understands, and casts those who witness it, as I have, into a state of questioning, whence one's delicate reality is scarce to escape intact and unscathed.

How do the footsteps of one who wets only his ankles in high water and carries in his skin and over his bones enough weight to make the bathroom scale read, "One at a Time, Please," walk one moment with thunderous steps, and the next scamper about in complete silence, as if lighter than air? How does a mind that functions as a plastic bag caught in a sweeping breeze fix its attention so ardently and with unwavering, laser-focused determination upon a single goal? How do dead, lifeless eyes follow the erratic trail forged by that which has captivated the plastic bag? And how does a handful of sausage fingers transform into the razor-lined mouth of a shark with prey-magnet teeth, snatching victims even out of midair?

Science says these things are not possible; yet, these things have I seen. They are not rare phenomena in the Connerian realm—again and again they set themselves on display, failing never to defy and amaze.

The Bloomdale Assassin, inspired by this real-life shepherd of the witless wanderer and impetuous inquirer, awaits your curious coming; and those based on the countless millions that have come before them, Zurmenz and Grezzy, stand by to carry you with them on this once-in-a-brief-lifetime journey of discovery and ultimate doom, in which the sharp eye might just catch the scent of a grander story lurking between the lines.

Onward!

On the wall

On the Wall
Office

"Hey, Buzz!"

"I told you four hours ago to stop calling me that. My name is Harold."

"Oh, c'mon! You've got to admit that's pretty clever! *Buzz-Buzz-Buzzzzz*—get it?"

"Yes, I get it, just like everyone else has gotten it since the beginning of time. And, no, I *don't* have to admit any such thing. It's trite, that's what it is—*trite*. Now, if you're through being a pesky pupa, I'd like to resume my present occupation."

"Aw, you Dumpstonians are all the same! You pompous pests think that having grown up in a walled community, feasting on Human scraps, somehow makes you better than everyone else! Well, just because I grew up on the back of road kill doesn't mean my wings hum any softer than yours!"

"Ha! That a Carrionite like you could even boast of his drone! Why, yours is so weak and imperceptible, I practically mistook you for a filthy Stench."

"How *dare* you! Your kind has the noisiest wings only because it takes a heck of a lot of flapping to lift those oversized thoraxes of yours after a whole day of grazing behind the restaurant in your precious dumpstervilles. And they're called Stoolians by those of us who have any hemolymph in our bellies!"

"Impressive! You know Human terminology, do you?"

"Oh, knock it off! It's not like Humans never venture into

the country."

"Yet, here you are."

"What? Am I not allowed to catch a whiff of sweet circle cakes and follow it wherever it leads, *Harold*? Honestly, when I knew you six days ago, you weren't nearly as pretentious and stuck up as you are now. We called you Zurmenz back then, remember?"

"I prefer Harold."

"Why? You're no Human. What is it with you Dumpstonians donning Human names?"

"We have a connection to Humans you simply could not understand. I was raised on their leftovers, the slime that drips from their very mouths onto half-eaten fluffy-white-mystery-smash-together delights. The essence of Humanity—*I* have *tasted* it!"

"And that makes you Human?"

"Of course not! But I understand them. And I don't hate them the way you country-dwellers do."

"We don't hate them! It's just, well...who do they think they are waltzing through our country and spraying that nasty-smelling stuff, huh? And, furthermore, did you know the ones who live out my way actually take pleasure in luring us to our deaths?"

"You mean like the myth of the Bloomdale Assassin?"

"Please—I'm not a maggot anymore. Seriously, there are Humans who use the most beautiful light you've ever seen to hypnotize us, drive us mad! They say once you get caught in the light, you go swiftly to your death."

"Have you ever seen these lights?"

"Have you even been listening? I just said that if you see them, you die."

"Well, then, I guess all you have is some wild conspiracy theory, then, huh? The Humans *I* know are a generous species; they fill our communities to the brim, and ask for nothing in return. Such bounty! Such generosity! Why shouldn't I adopt one of their names?"

"I often wonder if there's any hope at all for you. Maybe if you took the time to stoop to *my* level, take a quick trip on out to the country, you'd see the things I've seen. Maybe if you watched one of our own getting doused with that noisome cloud and then lie there helplessly on the grass, gazing hopelessly as help hovers just above, unable to swoop near enough to offer aid because of the repellant stink—maybe *then* you'd have a more rounded view of Humans and take pride in the name you were given."

"You're implying that your view is more rounded than my own. False; I am intimate with these creatures, as I have said; and I need not flutter about looking for country legends—if any are even rooted in a hint of truth—about what is most likely only a fringe populous of degenerates doing deplorable things."

"Whatever. There's no convincing you. Unless…"

"Unless, what?"

"Say the myth of the Bloomdale Assassin is true. Bloomdale isn't far from here. Say it's true, and say you saw him with your own eyes—would that change your mind?"

"If an outrageous larvae story like that ever came true before my very eyes, sure. Now, Grezzy, if you don't mind."

"Right. Circle cake time."

"Humans call them *doe'nuts*, Grezz—but that's not what's important here."

"Of course it is! They're beautiful! My proboscis is leaking just looking at them!"

"*Ugh*—so primitive! So uncultivated! Your kind can live out its entire existence thinking only of food! And what kind of life is that? There are riches far beyond sugary delights and decaying delicacies, you know…or, do you?"

"I used the word 'proboscis'—how uncultivated can I really be? Seems I know these Humans a little better than you're allowing yourself to believe. Don't chastise me because these *doe'nuts*, as you call them, aren't exactly falling out of the country sky, as they are in your walled world."

"Are you kidding? Humans throwing away doe'nuts? Now I *know* you're an ignorant, country fool! Had you any understanding at all, you'd know that doe'nuts are the prime fuel behind everything they do, everything they are!"

"Oh, knock it off!"

"Seriously! Doe'nuts make their world go round! It's like a dance, perfectly choreographed; and it goes around and around, in an endless cycle—until, of course, it ends."

"How so?"

"It's economic. Humans acquire the doe'nuts and eat them."

"Wow, Zurm—you just blew my mind…"

"That's step one—don't interrupt! Now, after eating their fill, as indicated by those straps they tie around their waists—you see them? Right, well, those things tell a Human when it should stop eating. Watch a whole meal, and you'll see them tugging at or unfastening them. Eventually, when they can no longer see the strap, due to its having been swallowed by the belly, they go to Humans in white coats who hold clipboards and dangle pendulums from their ears. These Humans—oh, wait… did I mention the green paper?"

"The what?"

"I see. Well, Humans can acquire doe'nuts only if they have green paper. They give it to other Humans in exchange for the doe'nuts."

"Do some Humans eat the paper?"

"Who can tell? I'm sure some do; although, with the way they pass it around, you'd think everyone and no one wanted it! Why, I've seen Humans chasing the green paper until they drop, only to hastily give it away!"

"Odd, for sure. So, what happens next?"

"Where was I?"

"White coats."

"Right. So, a Human goes to a white coat and offers green paper in exchange for being thoroughly examined, head to toe, and poked a great deal."

"Poked where?"

"Everywhere."

"They like this?"

"Hard to say, but all doe'nut eaters seem to follow this pattern. After this, the white coat gives them a map leading to a giant building where Humans go to cry—in exchange for green paper, of course."

"I don't believe it."

"You should see it! Dozens upon dozens of Humans with wet faces, throats screaming, bodies turning to jelly, water weeping from everywhere; and not one Human looks happy about it! I tell you, it's a house of self-torture."

"And just why would anyone do this?"

"As I understand it, they do it so that they might consume more doe'nuts."

"I don't get it."

"Aren't you listening? Doe'nuts are *everything* to a Human, but their bodies can hold only so much. Desperate to keep consuming, they use their green paper to get poked by white shirts and then torture themselves in those crying houses; and, while I don't quite understand the science, this frees up some space for more doe'nuts. Take this guy, right here, for instance—that strap around his waist. You can see it, no?"

"Already said I could."

"Now look at the other fellow. See his?"

"He's not wearing one."

"Ah! But he is! His belly is merely hiding it. See how the blue part of his body sits atop his legs like an upside down plume of smoke?"

"There's more body hiding under there?"

"Indeed! This one will soon be seeing a white coat and going to the crying house—mark my words!"

"But, if they both eat doe'nuts, why does *this* one's strap look like it's reluctant even to hug his waist?"

"It's the reason for the intrigue at hand. He hasn't adequate green paper, like the one sitting behind the desk. And he's trying to get some."

"How do you figure that?"

"Humans come to places like this to stare at the walls of a tiny room all day. Somehow, this creates green paper—strangely but surely. *This* frail thing will get his green paper in the same manner, which he can then use to get some doe'nuts."

"Staring at a wall makes green paper?"

"Yes, but not exclusively. I have also observed Humans fiddling about until they've manufactured something for which other Humans will offer green paper—if the thing is desirable, the paper is given to the Humans who manufactured it, who then give it to other manufacturing Humans, who keep passing it along, and…well, they get doe'nuts at some point."

"That's a dizzying circle—and there is *no* way you're correct. I mean, there are a TON of holes in what you've just spewed!"

"As is there a hole in a doe'nut! As the doe'nut is itself a circle! A circle about which these creatures dizzily dance! A sweet prize for which to live and die: their own life cycle…a circle! Round and round, with no need for a beginning or end, so long as it's sweet from the first bite to the last! If the bite is right, it's worth the fight!"

"Rhyming doesn't make it true."

"Try telling that to a Human. All their gods rhyme."

"This is ridiculous! Nothing of what you've said makes any sense! There's no way any of it is accurate."

"Like *you* would know better! I tell you, I learned this from one who had lived all of twenty-seven days!"

"Twenty-seven days! Impossible! No creature lives so long!"

"He had—he had! And it was he who'd introduced me to this place. Oh, the things he taught me! So, don't you start doubting my understanding of Humans! From doe'nuts to dirt they go! And, furthermore—wait…*shhh*! This is getting interesting."

"What is?"

"If the big one extends his hand, and the other one grabs it—"

"What? He'll get green paper for doe'nuts? If this Human had any sense, he'd forget grabbing hands, and instead grab one of the doe'nuts from THAT BOX RIGHT THERE! Honestly, I really think your grasp on Humanity is flawed."

"Your *wings* are flawed, Cark!"

"What did you call me?"

"You heard me!"

"Why, I aughta…"

"LISTEN!"

"To *WHAT*?"

"He just said it!"

"Said what?"

"The word."

"WHAT WORD?"

"I'd long thought doe'nuts were the key. But I've recently come to believe they are merely the reward: a reward attained via the only substance capable of animating these creatures."

"I'm leaving."

"The mother of all Human desires."

"Goodbye, Zurm."

"The breath of life, making possible all their frantic to-ing and fro-ing."

"Don't care—goodbye!"

"Their fuel. Their purpose. Their very being."

"Oh, for goodness' sake! WHAT?"

"*AXPRESSO*!"

"Huh?"

"The axpresso!"

"Is that a real word?"

"Humans say it all the time. Out by you they probably call it *kah'fee*. Ha! So primitive."

"I've heard of kah'fee, okay! And, no, smart stuff! They call it *cuppa'jo*, thank you very much."

"Whatever. My impassioned study of these creatures has led

me to this sacred fuel. And now I know I am near to cracking the code!"

"What code?"

"Humans! Haven't you ever wondered about them? Look at this one sitting on the bench just outside the window."

"Her? With the doe'nut glued to the back of her head?"

"That's hair."

"No. *That's* a doe'nut. It looks just like the brown one in the box—see?"

"It's hair, genius. And, actually, I think it's a *he*."

"Really?"

"Eh, who can tell? Anyway, you see how its leg is bouncing up and down? See the others through that window? See how they're just scurrying about?"

"So?"

"They can't sit still. *This* one wants to be like *those* ones out there! He—or, whatever it is—wants to be out there scurrying, as well. But he's not. He's here for the green paper. But the axpresso is already in his system. He's about to burst. Why?"

"You just said: because the axpresso is in his system."

"No! *Why*? Why all this scurrying? Why the need to be fueled, to be jacked up? Where are they going? Here and there—never slowing! Green paper for doe'nuts: it's all just a circle of energy, compounded by axpresso! What is their purpose? Why *are* they?"

"Wait…I thought you'd said doe'nuts were the primary fuel. You said earlier that doe'nuts are the very thing for which they live. So, you've contradicted yourself, and the mystery is solved. Now can we have some doe'nuts?"

"Are you kidding? My statement from earlier was one drawn

from evidence acquired over a great deal of study. It's been a whole ten minutes—give or take—since I spoke thusly: more than enough time to acquire new evidence and thereafter draw a new conclusion."

"Gosh, has it been that long? Wow, now that you mention it, you *do* look a lot older! How is it possible these Humans haven't changed a bit in all that time?"

"Knowledge passed down from generations has proven we live in a different realm than they do. Time affects us in different ways, which is precisely why I am engaged in my present study."

"Different realms? Different time effects?"

"Ours is a fast-paced time. The calculation, in relation of it to that of Humanity's, is just under a day for every minute."

"What?"

"Our minutes are like their days—roughly."

"That can't be right! It's been ten minutes—nearly ten days for them—and it's still the same day!"

"It's the *effect*! It's how time breaks upon the being, not that actual days are passing. No one can tell what an *actual* day is! Time knows only how to measure its days; we must draw from the comparison of realms to acquire the knowledge for our day-to-day...or, time-to-time...or, whatever! Anyway, by our calculations, if a Human were to live in our time realm, one of our days would cost them the equivalent of just over three of what they call a '*yeer*' in theirs; it's something like one thousand plus days—here, ten of *their* minutes costs you and me about eight days."

"Wait...who's paying for all this time? Do we age quicker, or do they?"

"Our time is faster—I've already said this. That's what makes this all so puzzling, so fascinating."

"I don't get it, Zurm. What's so fascinating?"

"*This*, my ignorant country-dweller, is the manifestation of the very fabric of another species. These rituals, like the one playing before us, are the key to unlocking the secrets of their purpose. Ten days—ten of *our* days, that is—I've studied them: a fascinating group. Why, I am compelled to wonder, if theirs is so abundant a time, do they hurry about as if trapped in *our* hourglass? We are born, we feed and breed, and we die—but they…*they* have such grander capabilities; and yet, they live like we do! Buzzing here and there, to and fro—always running, e'er on the go!"

"You rhymed again."

"Going, going, going; flitting, fluttering; pacing, prancing—dancing! Like us: always shooting about—they live like you and me! Or, do they? Why are they? What is their point? Indeed, they are cunning to conceal their ways; but I *will* crack the code. Before my time is through, I will finish the work our brethren have since the very first maggot strived to complete."

"Or, maybe—just maybe—you'll realize, as your wings twitch their last, that you'd spent your entire existence trying to unravel something that was, after all, not so complex. Honestly, you've already wasted over a third of your life! Can't you—?"

"Now, *there's* something new…"

"What? A revelation? A reality check? Haven't ever had one of those, eh? Well, maybe you should have a few—"

"I've never seen anything like it!"

"Wait…what?"

"Look, fool! *THAT*! What's happening? What is that thing? Oh, this is so exciting! Novel Human activity!"

"*That* thing?"

"Yes—the blackish thing that the big one just handed to the small one."

"You've never seen one?"

"*YOU* have?"

"Well, now! Is a filthy country-dweller the sole possessor of useful knowledge between this pair? Give me a second—I need to absorb this moment."

"You're about to lose a wing."

"Whatever—I've already stolen your pride."

"You've done no su—"

"We call 'em *poppers*."

"Poppers?"

"That's the noise they make—*POP*!"

"It makes noise? Why?"

"Well, that there is a small one. Some Humans have bigger ones."

"For what purpose?"

"How should I know? The big ones are so noisy, it's hardly worth sticking around when one is in use."

"How noisy?"

"Noisy enough to blow the skin off a deer."

"What? That's…*what*?"

"It's not just deer—I've seen it happen to rabbits, too; though, I can't say for certain what I *think* happened *actually* happened. You see, those times I've seen a Human walking around with a big popper, they're dressed in one of two colors: bright setting sun or earth; and every time there's a deer nearby—where *isn't* there a deer nearby, am I right?"

"Um…"

"Oh, yeah—Dumpstonian, over here. Anyway, I usually book it before the popper goes off; but when I return to the spot, I find the reason I routinely book it: a dead, skinless deer—or, as my folks would say, free real estate."

"You're saying the *sound* kills it? That's ridiculous! There are plenty of loud things out this way, and not one is fatal!"

"I've got plenty of family who were raised on such neighborhoods as a dead, sunbaked, and skinless deer, my friend. I know what I'm saying; you can mark the words of a filthy Cark like me."

"If *poppers*, as you call them, can do that to a deer, why have they no effect on the Human?"

"A mystery, no? Poppers seem only to animate Humans in a variety of ways."

"And what about small poppers, like this one?"

"Mostly see folk using them to topple tin cans and shatter glass bottles—lots of whooping and hollering goes on during such times. Never seen one skin a deer, and I've been near enough to them to know they're not fatal. I think they use them for parties—you know, for games, and stuff."

"So, this setting has turned into a game, has it? Interesting. And I assume that piece of paper being exchanged contains the instructions on how to play?"

"Maybe. What do you suppose those pictures are, the ones on the paper? Pretty weird-looking Human, that one; and what is—"

"Ooh! Green paper!"

"Wow, the small one got his green paper right away, didn't he? I thought you'd said Humans had to stare at a wall or make something first."

"In my observational experience, this is true—such has been the case in other places. But…this is rather curious. He *did* get that green paper rather quickly. And, look! There it is!"

"What?"

"The axpresso! That tall Human in black who just walked in handed them both an axpresso!"

"So, here we have a big Human with green paper, who, if he would grab the hand of the small one, would give green paper to the small one in exchange for his wall-staring or something-making, for which other Humans would want to exchange their green paper, so that the small one can use his green paper to get a doe'nut, like the ones behind him—but, instead of all that, the big one just handed over a stack of green paper, along with a popper and game instructions, before they both were given axpresso fuel, without an exchange of green paper. Oh, and look: the small one just grabbed a doe'nut."

"Now they've grabbed hands."

"You know, Zurm, as attentive and curious and fascinated as you are by these creatures, I really don't believe you have even the slightest clue as to their purpose, nor even the remotest understanding of their rituals. Now, what do you say we go and grab ourselves a doe'nut, eh?"

"It's Harold. And how about this: you stick with me today, and by the time the light fades, I'll have made you into a fanatic of Human activity—what do you say?"

"Deal. Doe'nut?"

"Absolutely. I'm starving."

Warehouse

"Get out of here! No way!"

"That's what he told me!"

"White powder? On the ground? Falling from the *sky*? C'mon, Zurm!"

"On the ground, in the air—oh, and he said the world becomes dark and that all its warmth vanishes."

"That's called night."

"No! Night during the *daytime*! It's like a lighter dark—a dayer night."

"I've never heard anything more idiotic."

"I'm telling you, he was really old and swore it was true—he had one eye, and was down to half a wing, too! Said the 'days of darkness' took them, along with everyone he'd ever known."

"Yes, and I've heard rumors of the green heads of trees becoming red before turning to ash—crazy talk! Just look around! Do you see any white powder or flaming tree heads? Are you dying from a world turned cold? Either of your eyes falling out? Wings secured?"

"Maybe the world itself changes."

"Doubtful. Now, what are we doing here? What is this place?"

"Ah, yes; well, Humans dislike using their legs."

"Nope! Sorry! You said that axpresso makes them want to move, and I saw that one Human's leg dancing like it wanted to be used. Your theory fails, once again!"

"Did you see any Human walking around today that looked

overfilled with doe'nuts?"

"Well, I—"

"No! You didn't!"

"It was a quick glance! How can I expect—"

"Humans have no problem walking when their bodies are empty—no doe'nuts in the belly means they're lighter! And the axpresso propels them to scurry in search of becoming heavier!"

"That tiny Human *was* rather small. Can't imagine he weighed much. Still, I'm sure I've seen a larger Human walking."

"They walk, but the big ones don't do it for long periods of time."

"I guess I've never timed any walking Humans. Still, why would they choose *not* to walk if they have legs with which to walk?"

"Something to do with the fact that their puny feet tire from supporting all that weight stored above. Such poorly designed creatures."

"That's a little irreverent for you, isn't it?"

"How so?"

"An hour ago, you seemed desirous of becoming a Human yourself; now you criticize their design."

"Keep up, Grezz. I told you I am immersed in study. How could one who studies for a whole hour come out the other end with the same thinking with which he began it?"

"I've heard tell that Humans do so; only, they spend countless days—and, probably, dozens of their so-called *years*—developing their stagnant minds."

"Yes, I know. They call it 'kahledge.'"

"Out my way they call it 'hyskule.'"

"Same thing, Grezz."

"That's what I'd figured. Why do they do that? Have different names for the same thing, I mean."

"Maybe they're as poorly designed in the head as they are in the body."

"You may be smarter than I'd like to admit."

"I need not your admissions to be assured of my mental capacities."

"Nor I yours for yours…"

"A labored insult, but I'll overlook the stretch and give you a pity point."

"ZURMENZ! What are we doing here?"

"Right. So, first of all, the name is Harold; and, second of all, Humans—pardon me—*big* Humans don't like to use their legs. But how do wingless beasts get around without the use of legs?"

"Zips."

"Your country tongue again?"

"No Human by us ever gave 'em a name, other than *pea'kup*; and that's a dumb name."

"*That's* the dumb name…right. Anyway, Humans call them *rides*."

"Like, the word ride?"

"Same word."

"Again with this weird word stuff! Only, now it's backwards! The *same* word for two *different* things?"

"We're learning a lot, aren't we?"

"Except for WHY WE'RE HERE!"

"I was just getting to that. See *him*, that guy down there? He's like a white coat for rides."

"Where's his white coat?"

"No white coats—blue shirts and mud."

"Mud? Why mud?"

"Do Humans out by you really travel atop horses?"

"Yes."

"Hmm…then I wonder if my theory is correct. I have long postulated that Humans coat the bottoms of their rides with mud to make the ride feel as though it's a horse."

"I don't follow."

"Well, horses can walk and run anywhere, yes?"

"I guess so."

"Right; but rides never deviate from the hard stone. Rides must see other means of Human transportation, like horses, walking on the earth; so, to keep them content with the hard stone to which they're confined, Humans take their rides to places like this to get mud slapped on them; rides are also thoroughly poked and examined here—the difference is the blue shirts."

"Nope. I've seen zips running through the mud."

"No you haven't."

"I care WAY less than you do about all this Human observation stuff—lying would be a waste of already idle brainpower."

"Then…if it's not mud, what is it?"

"Looks like you'll have to spend another quarter of your life to find out."

"I was so sure…you're not lying?"

"Nope. Just as sure as the Bloomdale Assassin hunts his prey, I'm a truthful little—"

"I knew it! I knew you were lying! I was right!"

"No you weren't—and aren't. I was kidding. But, you'd think a Human enthusiast like yourself would be a bit more curious about the Bloomdale Assassin."

"You're irritating me."

"Not even a *little* curious?"

"Even *you* said you didn't believe the story. Why should a Dumpstonian believe what even a Carrionite dismisses as fiction?"

"Whoa, now! There's a pretty low insinuation in what you just said!"

"Not quite as low as my opinion of *your* kind."

"And what is *my* kind? Am I so unlike you that we aren't even of the same species? Does my birthright and locality somehow separate us on a fundamental level?"

"Of course! Honestly, Carks like you just can't see the big picture. You're like these Humans: can't keep a straight line; here or there, wherever—it doesn't matter. You just scurry about, this way and that, around and around; you have no purpose, outside of your basic urges—feed, feed, feed, scurry, breed, and feed; just like *them*. Perhaps I should be studying *you*!"

"And what are *you*, then? You know *my* name—what's yours? What do they call things like you?"

"If you could but know how wretched you really are. Don't you think I can see over the treetops of our existence from where I stand?"

"Wow…"

"Maybe it's not your fault, you know?"

"My *being* is a fault?"

"Whatever it is, it's not me."

"Oh! So, *this* is why you've taken me with you, is it? You're performing a service! A service to a lowly, underprivileged, unfortunate, unfit-to-be, poor, poor, depraved, and deprived creature!"

"Can't do much serving with your constantly interrupting, now, can I?"

"You know what? I think I've just commenced a study of my own."

"Oh, really? Going to start paying attention, finally?"

"In more ways than you know."

"Good—because, that big Human is here."

"Which one?"

"The one from earlier: the one who gave the small one the green paper."

"What's he doing here?"

"Looks like another exchange of green paper. See?"

"So, does this zip belong to that big one?"

"Probably—I mean, why else would he…wait a second…"

"Where's he going?"

"You think *I* know? I'm surprised he's not still in his original habitat!"

"He just came here to give green paper for nothing? And, he's walking! Once again, your knowledge proves flawed! Seems the green paper *isn't* used transactionally! Seems we don't know what its purpose actually is! And, it seems all the more, that Humans walk regardless of size!"

"But, look! The blue shirt just picked up an axpresso and doe'nut from that table over there!"

"So what? He didn't use the green paper to get it! Maybe he grows axpressos and doe'nuts in the mud he paints on the zips."

"I thought you'd said it *wasn't* mud!"

"I thought you'd said it *was*!"

"Oh, I just don't get it! Why does it always happen that you go to present your hard-earned findings and complex discoveries, only to have a species as dumb and directionless as Humans foul up the works by spinning in circles?"

"Hey—check it out! That tall Human in black just walked in; the blue shirt left his doe'nut on the table."

"Let's hope it has some of those soft, multi-colored sticks on it."

"Try a blue one—makes the head delightfully fuzzy."

"I think you're becoming a bad influence on me."

"Just you wait."

"Not when there's a doe'nut involved. C'mon."

Restaurant

"One at a time?"

"Most often one, but two or three happens now and then, so I'm told."

"Wow. I guess Humans won't be around for very much longer, then, will they?"

"At this rate, Grezz, probably not. There just won't be enough of them to compete with species like ours."

"I just can't wrap my mind around that! I mean, my mother bred over one hundred of us in a single sitting! They can do just *one*? We're gonna dominate the world, soon—don't you think?"

"Every great species needs a leader; perhaps, he could be me."

"Good luck. I'm not sure even one of my brothers or sisters would submit to anything *you* told them to do."

"*You've* been following my lead all day! Regardless, that's not what I meant."

"You mean Humans?"

"Exactly."

"You want to be the leader of Humans? You want to be their sovereign? Zurm, Lord of Humans?"

"Of course! Only, it would be: *Harold*, Lord of Humans! I know their confused and erratic ways! I know how their spastic desires, which pull them this way and that, are the very sparks that animate the brain! And I know the nectar they so crave! With these tools, how could I be barred from taking over Human existence?"

"You think they'd submit without any resistance whatsoever? Moreover, to a *Harold*?"

"They may not even realize I've boxed them into my control."

"How so?"

"Their pursuit of satisfaction, of happiness: this is the key. If I can keep them pursuing, keep the doe'nuts and axpressos near enough to taste, yet just out of reach, they'll knock their heads silly against the wall of progress and go nowhere!"

"And how will you control all the necessary doe'nuts and axpressos?"

"Why, with hordes of loyalists! Creatures like you and me repulse and repel Humans, especially from foodstuffs! Therefore, we dominate the source, they stay away, and *we* decide which sources are left untouched and who will taste them—total control."

"So, they'll be able to see the thing they want, but they won't be able to reach it, unless you let them?"

"Exactly."

"And what if they don't trust their allotted portions?"

"What? Humans are dumb, but they're not *that* dumb! They'll savagely pounce on whatever I allow them to sample."

"Sounds like a wildly ambitions plan. Can't say I'm convinced."

"What hurdles can't I surmount? And who is there or will there be to stop me?"

"Ol' Bloomdale, maybe."

"Even *if* he existed, he'd be no match for me—he is, after all, Human, is he not?"

"I'd say not. He's hot air, spit from gullible mouth holes. So, to change the subject, what's so special about this place?"

"Ah, yes; well, Humans come here to choose mates."

"Looks like most have already chosen."

"So it would seem; however, the pairs you see here are not *actually* mates—not yet, anyway."

"And what does that mean?"

"They come here to stare at one another while they fill their faces with doe'nuts; afterward, they'll have a better idea as to whether they will produce offspring."

"Not everyone is eating doe'nuts. What is that stuff?"

"They eat strange portions before the doe'nuts—this is *my* country, don't forget; I was raised on the stuff set before them."

"I'm so glad I was raised on an opossum: no Human mouth ever touched *my* bed. I slept right where the zip's hoof had made a cozy dent in the temple of my home sweet beast."

"Fascinating. Now, look—there: you see that tall Human male with the scar on his cheek sitting across from that freckle-faced female? Like I said: doe'nuts and axpresso."

"Odd looking doe'nuts. They're all brown and sparkling—so shiny!"

"These are fancy doe'nuts; a lot of green paper is exchanged here."

"Hey! Look! See *that* guy? He's familiar, no?"

"Which one?"

"*That* one! Right there—the one with the plastic hair and tiny, shiny thing on his coat pocket; looks like one of those wavy, multi-colored things you see on top of buildings, doesn't it? See him? He's the one stuffing that stringy stuff in his mouth."

"Yes…he does look familiar. Where…"

"Oh! That picture! Remember? The big Human gave the small one the popper and a picture of *that* guy!"

"And, speaking of the small Human, there he is!"

"Where?"

"He just walked in the door! And he's got his popper with him!"

"Whoa! That one is loud! WAY louder than the ones country Humans use! It's like I've always imagined a big popper would sound! Only, were alive! How is it so loud, and yet not fatal?"

"Probably because these walls are trapping the sound—you've heard it only in the open air."

"Hey, you *are* smart, aren't you?"

"Yes, and I'll be deaf soon if that moron doesn't stop popping that thing."

"He can't pop it forever. They eventually run out of pops."

"Thus, you're proven right! I think we're both getting smarter. Gosh, he's in a hurry, huh? Didn't even stop for a doe'nut. Maybe he's run out of green paper."

"Where's the weird guy from the picture?"

"I think I saw him slip under the table. Boy, everyone is going NUTS!"

"Right! Just like I told you! Humans get REALLY animated over these popper things. Lots of whooping and hollering! Gracious, looks like an anthill down there! I've seen such colonies go absolutely crazy when a zip rolls over one—but this is WAY crazier!"

"Seems you speak and the world moves—look! That's the same zip we saw earlier!"

"So it is!"

"And, see that? He's already so tired of using his legs that he's desperately trying to get inside the zip and off his feet."

"You're still operating in flawed understanding, though—he's small!"

"Maybe the reason for zips is not yet wholly defined, but the fact is sure: Humans dislike using their legs."

"How funny is that? Quite a coincidence, no? You think that zip belongs to the small Human?"

"Guess so. I just wonder why we didn't see him at the—WOW!"

"DID YOU SEE *THAT*?"

"Why do you think I just screamed 'WOW'?"

"That zip just turned into the sun!"

"Who knew the sun was so loud? That was WAY louder than his popper!"

"I'll tell you what, Zurm, it's been a while since I've seen Humans make *this* much noise! Last time it was this noisy was just after I was born—they were making suns in the night sky until the real sun rose the next morning. It was SUPER loud! Can you believe we're alive?"

"Barely! This is getting to be a little much. What do you say we get out of here?"

"More places to go?"

"Sure!"

"Well, if you're gonna keep carting me around like this, I'm gonna need all the energy I can get."

"Sounds good to me. Hey—looks like that male and female left their fancy doe'nuts behind!"

"Shall we?"

"We shall."

Graveyard

"Hey, Buzz!"

"Harold."

"Gosh, it's been a long time, hasn't it?"

"I suppose so."

"You *suppose* so? Why, the last time I saw you we had just finished a few crumbs of a really fancy doe'nut, and were—"

"Three days ago."

"That was *three days* ago? Wow! We haven't crossed paths in *that* long? Guess we're just a couple of old-timers, now, huh? Three days…wow. Still studying your future subjects?"

"As you see."

"As I see—boy, lighten up, Zurm! Is this how you greet an old friend?"

"Friend?"

"Why don't you just rip off one of my legs while you're at it! What's with the attitude?"

"I'm working."

"You'd think three days would have been enough to change a guy."

"It was enough to get done a lot of work."

"Our lives are more than half gone, Zurmy! I've lived, I have! These last three days have been filled—FILLED, I tell you!—with such joys and adventures, as never one could imagine! And not *one* involved a Human. Yet, here you are: still trapped in the same rut in which I found you, long ago when we were young."

"If life has been so unbelievably magical, why have you come to waste it here with me? How, even, did you find me?"

"I asked around—eventually stumbled upon a bloodsucker who'd seen you whiz by earlier today. You know, you should really reach out to the bloodsucker community; they're pretty intimate with Humans, seeing as Humans are basically their diet. Anyway, I've searched for you all this time, from dawn until the falling of the sun; and you ask *why*! Indeed, why would I cast into the fire a whole day of my life, wander to and fro for so long, just to find *you*?"

"Repeating my question is not an answer."

"Maybe I don't know why."

"Maybe. Probably. Now, is there something you want? I'm very busy."

"I'd like to talk with you, Zurm—let's say, for the sake of old times."

"Talk *to* me; I can't promise I'll contribute enough conversation to warrant a *with*."

"We're presently operating at *with*; I'll bet I can maintain it. So, what's the story today?"

"Human activity."

"Silly me. What are they doing?"

"You heard the male just now, did you not? He's resting, Grezz."

"Who's resting?"

"The one encircled by the other Humans."

"Humans stand around to watch each other sleep? How odd. Besides, that's not a Human; that's merely a picture of—hey! That picture! Isn't that the face of the weird guy from the fancy doe'nut place? Guess he went under the table to go to sleep, then, huh?"

"This seems to be a different kind of sleep, for not all Humans sleep in places like this, or in big boxes like that. But, yes—after your sudden departure that night, I returned to find he was indeed asleep. Some Humans in a big, flashy ride carried him out of the place on a bed. I have followed him ever since, as his slumber seemed to be most interesting to the Humans around him. And so it has been; Humans have done some seriously bizarre things to try and wake him these three days, even going so far as to remove and replace his insides. Yet, still he sleeps. Eventually, I followed them to a white room, where he was placed in this box."

"The weird guy is *in* that box?"

"I once met a ripple wing."

"Did you? Now, how about we return to the story at hand, Zurm?"

"I wish you'd stop calling me that."

"What? Your name?"

"My name is Harold."

"Where did you ever dig up such a dumb name?"

"As I was saying, I once met a ripple wing, who claimed to have once been something like a hairy worm."

"*Katoorpillor* is what Humans call them."

"So, you're familiar with the concept?"

"Sure! I've known many a katoorpillor with ripple wing dreams, and I've known many a ripple wing with such tales to tell about his transformation from grub to glory."

"Well, *this* is, I think, the Human version. They tuck themselves into these boxes, and emerge later as something better—what that something is, I'm not sure. It must take a great long while, and I wonder if any Human has achieved ripple wing status; for all the Humans I see are equally, well, Human."

"What's that stuff on their faces?"

"Not sure, Grezz. It looks like rain, but we're inside."

"Do you think Human eyes are like clouds?"

"A rather strange conclusion; but, maybe."

"So, why is everyone just standing around? And why is everyone wearing the same color?"

"Human rituals really are a mystery; that's why we're here. Do you recall passing a field of stones on your way to this place? Some Humans don't even go to sleep inside—they put some in the ground."

"Like, beneath the grass?"

"Yup."

"Then, why is *he* in here?"

"I've heard them call it a *Moss And Leave Em'*. Based on how I've heard such words used, they must have covered him in moss before putting him in the box, after which they'll just, as the name suggests, leave him."

"Sleeping underground must be easier, then, no? Don't even have to bother covering the sleeping guy in moss—bct there's a lot of it down there."

"Could be. I've never been below ground. Though, I suppose it—"

"WOW! LOOK AT *THAT*!"

"Look at wha…? Whoa…"

"What is it?"

"I…I…it's so…so…beautiful…"

"I've never seen such…"

"*Blue*…wow…"

"It's…it's…it's just…oh, n-no…*no*…NO! NO! NO! ZURM!

WAKE UP!"

"*Shh*! I…I need to…"

"The *lights*! Zurm, cover your eyes!"

"There's so many of them…I must…"

"NO! C'MON! WAKE UP!"

"OUCH! Why'd you do *that*?"

"Just keep facing *this* way—don't look back!"

"What happened? Where are we?"

"Zurm, the lights! *THE LIGHTS*!"

"What lights?"

"Remember all those days ago, when I told you about the lights Humans would use to trap us?"

"It's been a whole three days since then, Grezz! You expect me to remember details from *that* long ago?"

"I told you that Humans hung these lights to hypnotize us and drive us mad! To kill us! Beautiful lights, they are! These must be the lights! Look! This wall is like water: you can see a reflection—see the lights?"

"Oh, my goodness—you're right! Wow…they really *are* beautiful!"

"Strange, isn't it? Those lights nearly sucked us into our doom! Yet, in this water wall, the temptation is minimized. Still, we probably shouldn't gaze too long. Let's get out of here."

"Wait! Look at them!"

"What?"

"You said the lights were produced by Humans, just as we see here—but you also said that they were created to hypnotize and kill *us*, right?"

"Yeah."

"Then why do all these Humans gaze helplessly into those

lights, themselves? Look at them! *Look at them*! Isn't it fascinating? Each has his or her own light, fitting nicely in the hand and shining its captivating blue light into their eyes—see how wide they are? The light reflects well off their orbs of white. That which they designed to control us actually controls them! Grezz, are you *sure* these lights were forged to kill *only* us? Who uses them? Where have you seen them?"

"I told you: I'd never seen them. It was all rumors; those who've seen them have died."

"Yet, here we are."

"So we are, thanks to me! I barely resisted and saved your buzzy behind!"

"Harold has found a way."

"What kind of a way?"

"We need to get one of those lights."

"Are you crazy? Even if we could transport one, how would we resist its power? And what would we even do with it?"

"If I can get my legs on that power, I can enslave all Humanity!"

"*Enslave*? What's gotten into you?"

"Not even the likes of the Bloomdale Assassin could stop me!"

"You *are* mad! Zurm, snap out of it! You can't take over Humanity! Being what you are, what *we* are, what *they* are—it can't be done! And it's foolish! Who would want to control such a pathetic species anyway?"

"I can make this world the way I want it to be! Their habits and proclivities won't be able to affect me any longer!"

"Their habits and proclivities are the only reason Dumpstonians like yourself are even alive! You were raised on the bounty of their waste! They are *literally* the hand that feeds you!"

"And under my control, I shall never again know hunger!"

"You never have!"

"Then, let me say I do it for you, for the Carrionite and the common Stench, that none should ever have less than I can give!"

"It's *Stoolian*! And who are *you* to think you could wield such power?"

"Who are *you* to say I can't?"

"Even if you were capable, 'could' and 'should' are two different things! I think you're blurring the two, and mixing in a heap of insanity!"

"Mad, am I? Why, then, let us put my madness to the test!"

"Zurm…"

"Let us dive headlong into the pit of madness!"

"*Zurm…*"

"You said you found me by way of the direction given from a passing bloodsucker, did you not? We'll rustle up a bunch of his buddies from the surrounding lake and puddle communities, and with their combined strength snatch one of these lights from one of these Humans—that tall one with the gleaming blue eyes, perhaps: won't have to exert too much energy to regain cruising altitude once we've taken it, given his lofty stature. And then—yes, then!—we'll put my insanity on trial! Let's go!"

"Hold it! Even if you *could* get bloodsuckers to focus on taking something other than blood from a Human—you can't—you'd need tens of thousands, probably, to muster the strength required for such a feat!"

"You're right."

"I am. Glad to see you're—"

"We need energy."

"What?"

"Look—over there: doe'nuts and axpresso. Let's grab a quick bite before we go."

"You know what? Let's. Maybe the sustenance will bring your spinning brain back to reality."

"Not that I value your insight as anything by which to draw a practical path, but you really think the union of our kind and bloodsuckers won't be enough?"

"A most pleasantly-worded insult, that was; and, yes—but, more than that, it can't happen. Like I said, you'd need an army far greater than you're likely to rustle up around here, and in enough time to achieve your aim. I mean, who knows how long these Humans are going to stick around."

"Oh! Darn it all! Again, you speak and the world moves! Where are they going?"

"Someplace else where mindless labor awaits them. Shut up and eat."

"But...oh, well. At least we've got a sludge-filled doe'nut here."

"Once again, you demonstrate your dependence on Humanity."

"Hmm? How so?"

"Do you realize that you'd never taste that sweet, red sludge had not a Human's jaws ripped open that doe'nut's skin?"

"Why do you think the idea of controlling them is so appealing? I'd have all the sludge gates opened at my will!"

"Or, they'd seal their jaws."

"Impossible. Their need for a bite of their own is too great to be ignored. Even if a lag in control was possible, it would be only a matter of time before I buried my face in sludge."

"You know, some of us spend a lifetime working toward the sludges beneath layers far less sweet than a doe'nut's."

"Poor souls. Why expend the effort when something else can do it for you? Work with the head, not the body."

"Some of us feel the sludge is all the sweeter when laced with toil—our labor makes the reward more worth the earning."

"Ridiculous. You'll waste your life waiting. Taste it while you can, I say! Who cares about the means employed?"

"Maybe so. How about passing a glob of sludge my way?"

"*What*? Find your own doe'nut!"

"Ha! Oh, Zurmy, Zurmy—you have indeed brought a bit of color into this life. What shade is that color has yet to be seen, I'm sure; but it is a color, nonetheless. We'll see what sludge awaits me in my own doe'nut, here."

"Knock yourself out."

"Gladly. Feeling better, now that you've had a few slurps of sludge?"

"Loads better! At last, I think I'm thinking clearly."

"You think? If you're thinking clearly, why the doubt?"

"I mean, I *am* thinking clearly."

"Mhmm."

"Yes, this has been a most enlightening experience, and a most invigorating meal."

"I'm glad to hear it."

"Indeed—yet, there exist still more unsolved Human mysteries."

"Many more, I'm sure."

"Though, few quite so enticing as one."

"With all the behavior to which you have made me a witness,

it's hard to imagine anything more Humanity can offer to pique my interest."

"I confess, the study of Humans has become a tad tired to me—many of those mysteries could not, to use your words, *pique* my interest, either."

"I find that hard to believe, Zurm. You? Really? Bored with solving the Human mystery?"

"Certainly! I feel I've learned just about everything one needs to know in order to take control of the race; now, I'm bored. Soon, I'll be at the apex of the Human world, leading Humans about by the nose, as they gaze into my lights."

"Which you have yet to determine how to wield."

"A minor detail. The 'what' of the matter is known—the 'how' will soon follow. Anyway, as I was saying, there at the helm of Humanity will I be; and I'll look down upon my empire and realize that there remains no excitement to be had in my remaining days. If all Humanity is under my control, I will face no challenge, whatsoever. Thus, the boredom that fills me now will be compounded."

"Life moves quickly, Zurm. Perhaps, you're micro-focusing—there's an even greater world out there, you know? I've seen it! I've lived in it! And from it have I taken plenty to carry me to the last."

"I once saw a giant animal in the home of a Human."

"Sometimes I wonder if you even hear me, much less listen to me."

"It was enormous! It looked like other animals I've seen; only, it stood well into the ceiling and bore a ferocious snarl upon its face that neither moved nor made any sound. At first, I wondered why the animal stood so still, why it used not its mighty claws and humongous teeth to tear its way into your country, where I assume it belonged."

"I've never seen something quite as big as you have described! It was standing, you say?"

"Standing, snarling—still and silent; it had shiny, blue eyes, and very bushy, soft hair, covering it from snout to heels; and when Humans entered the room, it still would not move, nor snatch for itself a meal."

"Odd. Very odd. And, you rhymed again."

"One of the Humans stood fearlessly before this thing, pointing at it with a stiff finger; the other Humans gaped. Still, the creature remained still."

"This is so strange! Why did it not move?"

"I think now I know why, thanks to you."

"Me?"

"I did not realize it until today. That creature, Grezz, stood on a platform of wood; and above its wide, unwavering eyes, was a bright light, gazing directly back at it."

"You mean…"

"Humans might be a tad more cunning and capable than I have come to believe; for what can be said of a creature who can set beneath its control another creature more than twice its size, bearing resources, such as claws and teeth, that would otherwise make the confrontation a no-contest?"

"Truly mindboggling."

"Inspiring, is the word I would use. And therein lies the challenge, the only challenge creatures like us have left in this world: to tame the giant among Humans, just as Humans have tamed the giant among animals."

"Quite a task, I'd say. And, if I'm being perfectly honest, a tad intriguing. Oh, heck—I guess it *does* sound exciting! Though I can't say I share your motives, taking command of a Human giant would certainly be a convincing blow and status-securing feat. Still, one must wonder where to go to find such a giant."

"You thinking what I'm thinking?"

Bloomdale

"This is not what I was thinking."

"It *does* exist…"

"Bloomdale? Of course it exists, Zurm! Have you really *never* been more than half a day's flight from Dumpstonia?"

"I…I didn't really…that is…"

"Oh, come *on*! Are you—are you trembling? Your wings are twitching!"

"I'm not trembling! My body is just preparing for the rigorous task ahead! This *twitch*, as you call it, is just my wings loosening up for what might be a great exertion!"

"The trip to this place didn't loosen them?"

"The trip has left them cramped!"

"Cramped wings?"

"It's possible!"

"Possibly. Now, let's get out of here, huh? No use wasting our time chasing—"

"What? *Leave*? COWARD!"

"Excuse me? The word is *realist*! There's nothing to be found here, Zurm."

"HAROLD!"

"GIVE IT UP!"

"Bloomdale, or my *real* name?"

"Both! Look, this is just an old house, okay? All that stuff about the assassin is just talk."

"'*The way is open, the gate*…um…is, um…*also open*…'"

"It's nothing more than a good story to scare the maggots!"

"'*Don't be shy. Step*…uh…*inside.*'"

"Oh, for goodness' sake! Are you trying to recite the Assassin's Scrawl?"

"Not trying—*am.*"

"*Aren't.* You've got it all wrong."

"Hey! It's a long piece, if I remember correctly; furthermore, I haven't heard it in at least fifteen days, so…"

"And here you are: so confident that you can tame the most famous creature of fiction, and you can't even properly recall the words of the story!"

"I know the gist of it!"

"That's not enough to know your foe—much less make him real!"

"I don't suppose you could recite it."

"Not at all! I don't waste my time with frivolity!"

"Yet, here you are."

"Point. I'm leaving."

"Wait!"

"WHAT?"

"Just this once—"

"Nope! I've given you a lot of 'onces'."

"Okay, then, just this *last* once. C'mon! Let's uncover this mystery together! Even if there's nothing here to find! Let's give the Human experiment one last go!"

"How has this been an experiment? We've done nothing but observe."

"Whatever! C'mon! Please! I'll get you a doe'nut."

"No you won't—you can't."

"I'll help you find one…in this house—c'mon! Where are you going?"

"Goodbye, Zurm. I hope you don't end up feeling that you've wasted—"

"Wait! Grezz! Wait!"

"Not waiting! Bye!"

"No! Stop! Grezzy!"

"AHHH! What was that? Where are we?"

"You idiot! You flew right through the door! Oh…wow! WE'RE IN THE BLOOMDALE HOUSE! This is incredible!"

"You're celebrating? How the heck did we get in here?"

"You tell me!"

"The air smelled good this way—I thought, not a bad way to go, right?"

"I agree!"

"I don't!"

"Look at this place!"

"Hey! Where's the door?"

"You're right. Wasn't the outside just here a second ago? Gosh, it's dark in here. I could have sworn this was a door; it feels like a wall."

"It looks like a wall."

"It must be a wall."

"How do we get back outside? Zurm! How do we get out of here?"

"You expect *me* to know? I hardly remember the Scrawl!"

"Speaking of the Scrawl…*look*—that big wall, right over there."

"No…"

"It can't be…"

"I don't believe it…"

"Is it really?"

"No, no, no, no! It can't be! Grezz, tell me it's not what it looks like it is!"

"If I wasn't scared to death, I'd pound you for being such a big-talk coward! You were going to waltz right in here and tame the mythical beast! Well, Zurmenz, here's your beast!"

"These words…can you read them?"

"Of course not! Besides, there's barely enough light to—"

"*Shh*! What's that?"

"I don't—"

"*SHHHHHHH*!"

"Why you—hey; I *do* hear something! It's coming from down there!"

"Go closer! Tell me what it is!"

"Why don't you—oh, never mind!"

"Go! Go!"

"Zurm! Get down here! Hurry!"

"What is it? What's—*AHHH*!"

"Quiet! He's barely alive! He's trying to whisper something!"

"What's he saying?"

"Hush! Listen!"

Upon the hill, in Bloomdale Land,
Resides the world's most lethal hand.
As lightening striking: 'tis his touch;
His feet are swift and silent; clutch
Doth he thy dressing for the tomb,
To sop the innards of fools, whom
Have heard his name and come to call;
How pride doth go before the fall!
To 'scape the heat, to catch a whiff,

To see the sights, to test the cliff,
To idly drift, to grab a bite,
To see for once, to follow lights;
To know the truth behind the tales,
To search the heights, explore the vales;
To test his power, patience, will;
To tempt his thirst, behold his skill;
To find a new frontier to roam;
To stumble forth, so far from home;
To realize how lost you are,
To take with thee Death's mortal scar,
And find for thee a lasting end;
Come hither! Welcome, foolish friend!
The way is broad! The gate spread wide!
Be not afraid; come; slip inside.
Find rest. Peace. Respite. Desire;
Meadows for beds and wood for fire.
Be still. Be silent. Noiseless. Mute.
Scream not; don't cry, holler, or hoot.
Do not twitch. Don't breathe. Just stay still.
I hear your wings. I sense my kill.
The day you see is phantom light.
There's no escape; I am the night,
Which comes to snatch thee from the air:
The Hand of Death; your worst nightmare.
Beat 'gainst the phantoms; twirl in place;
Sail to and fro; I'll win this race!
The gate is sealed. The way is shut.
Once and for all you'll learn just what
Has lurked in legend, fiction, myth,

And comes to show himself, forthwith!
'Tis I!
The deal for real, your fate to seal,
O, yes! 'Tis I! See 'neath the veil!
I, the Assassin of Bloomdale!

"IT'S THE SCRAWL, GREZZ! He's speaking the Assassin's Scrawl!"

"And these etchings above must be the very words."

"If the Scrawl exists, if *this* is it, if this poor creature of our kindred speaks it plainly as he lies dying…the Assassin must also exist."

"More than that, he may be near."

"More than that—IT'S HIM!"

"HE'S HERE!"

"He's seen us! He's coming!"

"Zurm! Quickly! To the heights! Soar beyond his reach!"

"Let's go! He'll never be able to—THE LIGHTS!"

"Cover your eyes! DIVE! DIVE!"

"Grezzy! Where are you? GREZZY!"

"I've got you! Just keep going!"

"Where? We're sailing blind!"

"Better than sailing dead! Just beat the air! Go! Go!"

"OUCH! What did we hit?"

"No time to wonder—do you see the Assassin?"

"THERE! I see him!"

"Okay, good! He's looking the other way; so, let's use this opportunity to scour for a passage to the outside."

"Oh, Grezz! Listen! He's chanting the Scrawl!"

"Calm down!"

"Those lights came out of nowhere!"

"Must be part of the Assassin's trap—looks like he keeps them hidden in the rafters to draw our kind to our deaths. Clever, keeping us in the dark."

"Clever?"

"Think about it! Our instincts tell us to soar beyond his reach, right?"

"Well, yours did, thankfully."

"Sure; so, knowing this, a skilled hunter—as legend has asserted him to be—would use our instincts against us. By acting in accordance with what we feel is safe, we sail straight into his trap: the lights. Boy, if we hadn't acted quickly, we'd be—"

"Oh, my goodness…"

"What?"

"Look…by the Scrawl."

"Oh, poor fellow!"

"The Assassin has finished his work."

"Listen, Zurm, we're not going to end up like him, all right? We're going to make it! We're going to get out of here!"

"But…the Scrawl says there's no escape! '*The gate is sealed. The way is shut.*' Remember?"

"And how do you think those words were ever used to lull us to sleep when we were maggots?"

"I…I don't know."

"Someone passed them along, Zurm! One of our kind *must* have escaped, meaning the Assassin has not a perfect record. We can beat the odds! We'll be the ones telling the tale from now on, recounting a firsthand experience, rather than a myth!"

"But I don't *want* a firsthand experience!"

"You've *got* one! Whether you want to admit the reason why, you have got one! Listen to me, now; the air is different in here than it was outside. If we can find a stream of outside air, it might lead to a crack or a crevice—something just big enough through which to squeeze ourselves."

"How are we going to find one?"

"We've got to keep moving."

"But I don't *want* to move!"

"Not an option for the living, Zurm! We're at ground level; we should try to hover out of reach of all appendages. Right now the feet are a threat; too high and there's the lights; his arms also have a lot of range—we should try to keep to knee-level."

"Look at him—how grotesque! He's examining his kill! And still chanting! OH! Is he grinding it in that cloth? *OH! Mercy!*"

"He sure lives up to his legend. He'll be after us next; we need to get moving."

"But he doesn't know we're here, does he? Why don't we stay?"

"You would linger in the belly of the beast, all to avoid the threat of death? We've got to get moving!"

"I can't, Grezz! I'm scared!"

"So am I! But now is not the time for fear! Whether now or later, he'll find us! This is *his* domain! Does not the prince of this realm know better the landscape we must navigate? He knows the place we hide; he needs only return to it and find us sitting helplessly to fulfill the promise of his Scrawl. We have no better chance than to disentangle ourselves from this place!"

"You're right. Oh, my goodness! I don't know if I can do this!"

"You can. You must. Pull yourself together. We go when the danger is most near."

"WHAT?"

"If we wait until he's right on top of us, we can slip past him and leave him a greater distance to follow."

"*IF* we can get past him! What if we wait only for him to scoop us up because we waited?"

"We'll make it, Zurm!"

"No! We go now! There! Soft light in the corner—looks like outside! Let's go!"

"That's the spirit! *C'mon*!"

"He hasn't seen us yet! Go! Go! Go!"

"Right behind…hey…wait a second—I've seen him before, haven't I?"

"Keep up, Grezz!"

"A tall Human."

"Lot's of Humans are tall!"

"Draped in black."

"They dress in all sorts of colors!"

"With a scar on his cheek."

"Even Humans are fragile!"

"And gleaming blue eyes."

"Wait, *what*?"

"Him! The Assassin—we've seen him before!"

"I don't believe it! The Human who'd delivered the axpresso!"

"The one who'd met with the blue shirt!"

"The one sitting with the freckle-faced female!"

"The one holding a light in the *Moss And Leave 'Em*!"

"IT'S HIM!"

"He's seen us! Go, Zurm! Go!"

"We're almost there! Just a few more—OUCH!"

"No! What is this? What is it? Isn't this the outside?"

"It is, but why can't we get there! It's a wall, but I can see the outside! What is it?"

"Oh, my goodness! It's one of those water walls! Like the one we just saw, remember? Look! I can see myself!"

"I can see me too! And…GREZZY!"

"AAAAARRRRRRGGGGHHHHH!"

"GREZZY! NO!"

"Uhhhh."

"I've got you! C'mon, Grezz! We're getting out of here! Hang on, buddy!"

"L-leave m-me…I-I'm too…too heavy to ca-carry."

"I've got you! Just hang on a little longer! He got us, but we're not dead yet!"

"D-don't…just g-go…save…save yourse…"

"No! No! Stay with me! I'm going to set you down here, okay? I don't think he can reach this high. Maybe there's something I can use to…oh, Grezz."

"I w-won't make it…Zurm. This is it…he g-got me."

"He hasn't! Not while I have strength left."

"Harold…"

"Grezz?"

"Harold…you're a g-good frie…friend."

"But I'm not! I'm the worst kind! It's *my* fault we're even here!"

"I thought y-you were j-just ano…another ignorant Dumps…stonian. I was wr…wrong, Harold."

"My name is Zurmenz…remember? You taught me that."

"I t-*told* you that. You…you've made…made it so."

"I'm going to get you out of here."

"D-don't bother. I ha-have over one hun…hundred maggots

who wi-will carry me f-far from this pl-place…in their very be…being, they…will ca-carry me."

"I've stolen you from them, Grezz. I'm so sorry."

"I ra-raised them well. They were on th-their own long bef…before I came looking f-for you. My labor for th-them is over; it w-was you I needed t-to reach."

"I'll never forget you, Grezz. I'm sorry I was a stubborn fool until the end."

"It wa…wasn't too late. You're a new cr-creature, and—*heh*—it was sure a qu-quick meta…morpho…sis."

"We live in quick time, don't we?"

"Ve-very quick."

"You told me to wait until the danger was near on purpose, didn't you?"

"Ha…"

"You let me figure it all out for myself."

"I knew you wo-would. Wasn't t-too late. Good…goodbye, old f-friend."

"Goodbye, dear Grezzy. And now, Assassin—'tis but you and I! What a clever trap indeed you have laid! And there *is* no escape! But you will remember *this* creature above all the rest! As you draw breath, so shall you draw *me*! Spread wide the gate, Assassin! Draw the killing breath! Zurmenz is on his way! His final flight, soaring through the narrow fray! For Grezzy, the dead, and those you've yet to kill! Right or left is now the choice! For glory, good riddance—THE GAPING NOSTRIL!"

REPORT

This has been an official recording of two key eyewitnesses to the assassination of party leader Brian Altier (ΛIB). The transcript contained herein has been translated to the best of the state's ability, employing dozens of insect experts and insectan linguists to ensure this document presents the most accurate representation of the facts. Witnesses were placed under recorded surveillance per federal order 0991-72-20.

Subjects A (aka Zurmenz, aka Zurmy, aka Zurm, aka Buzz, aka Harold) and B (aka Grezzy, aka Grezz) are classified as material witnesses to many of the events leading up to Altier's assassination at Chachiano's Restaurant on the evening of July 21, 2017. The state is presently reviewing the connections of these events.

Both witnesses are presumed deceased.

Note: The entirety of this eyewitness testimony is submitted into evidence as exhibit No. 27.

END REPORT

Prologue: Violinist

AS we approach the conclusion of this second book of Ramblings and I look ahead to those forthcoming (if any), permit me, if you will, to say that I have enjoyed my time conversing with you, dear reader. One-sided though our conversations must be in this medium, I feel, in a most peculiar and wonderful way, that my office has served to draw the holder of the pen closer to those who ingest its fruits.

Ever do I wrestle inwardly with my identity, my nature—wondering whether my existence serves not to enrich the work of my employer, but rather to detract from it, to create a tonal dissonance that would undermine with levity what are mostly weighty stories, the messages of which are dear to the artist's heart. I believe that Conners tolerates me for two primary reasons (and these I have not verified with him, nor will I for fear that the more accurate count of said reasons will be proved fewer): first, that you, dear reader, are under no obligation to read what is filtered through my voice and onto the page; and second, that a not insignificant part of Conners' complexion is humor, is the undermining of the severe with the lighthearted, is the inconsistency in tone; for he, like all of us, is not merely one thing. It was for this reason that he formed Route 27 Publishing®—other reasons aside, when he was informed by a publisher that he would have to "pick a lane," establish his name under a specific genre, he declared that he simply could not! One day he is inspired to write literary fiction, the next he is soaring through the cosmos with a tale of science fiction; then he's off on a grand, fantasy adventure, before settling down with few words for an easy, children's read. It may make him less marketable, but anything else would be less genuine. And what, then, would be the point of writing?

Conners was told once by a book editor that the fewer the words, the more important each word is. This has not since dissuaded him from waxing over-eloquently upon the page, as perhaps you have noticed; but it speaks well to this next story. In but a few pages, Conners sought to capture a fleeting, fragile moment, employing no more words than were absolutely necessary to paint the scene and pierce the heart with the potency embedded therein.

Violinist

NAUGHT but the low, throaty call of the horn was heard over the vacant land that before my sleepless eyes lay dry and splintered, heavy laden with a blinding fog, its branching fissures mimicking the barren boughs and vacant arms littered about the scene, becoming crimson rivers emptying into lakes of pitch, whence the earth could draw nothing to revive its life, as it gluttonously reclaimed the dust that was to it returning.

As the horn faded into nothing, taking with it the passage of time, I heard the beating of drums thumping hard—two pounding beats, together, controlled; and not another pair to join them until the echo of the first had passed away. All across the trench they thumped, keeping to this intense pattern of pounding and pausing, as if the drums did sound to maintain their presence, pumping notes so violent that their music might keep the instrument alive for yet another beat, while in the stillness of the vanishing echo the ear could listen for an answer to the burning question, an answer that lay just beyond the veil of fog, growing ever thicker.

I had not known him before, nor can I say that I remember his name. That name is, to me, recalled only in the peace he did from his instrument sing in that hour, when the fog was for but a moment—one glorious, eternal moment—parted, and the gloom of our unending day forgotten.

Like me, he was not born to wear the shoes we were called to fill, nor bear the burden we were called to bear. No man is born for such work; its fruit is toxic and its harvesting unnatural. Yet man seems never to cease sowing the poisonous seed, nor does he tire from reaping. And like men were we called to cast aside the instruments of music and take up instruments of mourning, the kind that seem never to leave the hand nor cease to peal, even when they are silent and silenced.

"The chorus will play, even without me," he said, as we lay there, pressed against the earth, our eyes to the ledge above us, beyond which grew the fog. "But all of myself will I lay down, that perhaps the note I have been given to play will be remembered."

Across the silent world cut the low, throaty call of the horn. And, in an instant, he was gone, the disorganized din of the orchestra roaring over my head.

Naught but the low, throaty call of the horn was heard over the vacant land that before my sleepless eyes lay dry and splintered, heavy laden with a blinding fog, its branching fissures mimicking the barren boughs and vacant arms littered about the scene, becoming crimson rivers emptying into lakes of pitch, whence the earth could draw nothing to revive its life as it gluttonously reclaimed the dust that was to it returning.

As the horn faded into nothing, taking with it the passage of time, I saw him once again, breaking through the ever-thickening fog, his head bare, his face dirtied, his clothes stained with streaks and splotches of black and crimson, staggering, while to his arm cleaved another like him, like the rest of us.

Having made it to the ledge, he and the other slid down into the pit where we stood, while several rushed to attend to the paled man, who dropped to the mud in a heap, his lips whispering a breathy dirge, one we had all before heard many times.

Stepping from the man he had carried across the waste above, the man I remember stepped silently, slowly to the opposite side of the trench, where he released from his shoulders the pack that he had taken with him into the noiseless fog. Setting it gently into the mud below, he carefully, ever so gently, extracted from it an old violin and bow.

Pristine it was not, for no proper case could he give it; even the bow was slightly frayed. Nevertheless, he nuzzled the instrument under his chin, set his fingers upon the strings, and placed the bow atop them; then, drawing silent stream of air through his nose, his eyes softly sealing, he began to pull.

The notes were not perfect, the sound impure; many times the instrument let out a screech or a cough—but there had never been a tune so beautiful or music so moving. With every ounce of his passion, he waltzed with the bow across the rusted strings; and as the fog above, about, and within us parted, and from without the sun did shine forth as never it had since the day we'd arrived, all the earth stopped to listen.

On he played, never once opening his eyes or releasing himself from the music that he had been given to translate into our hearts, conveying this divine message: that though this world may wade about in darkness and we, through the filth of our ways, are made to trudge, those who know the Son of God, the Maker of Music, are but passing through this wasteland and will, in but a little while, be lifted from the fog, ever into light.

And when the grand instrument had sung its last vibrato, he laid down the bow, the violin, and then himself, though the sweet tremors he had from the strings caressed echoed long after that day, even in those who had heard it, whichever side of the trench he called his own.

Outro

OVER a year ago, upon conclusion of the seven stories of Ramblings One, I endeavored, albeit facetiously, to tie together each tale by the rope of a common theme—or, to use the terminology employed in that text, I stuffed each story into the meatball of life—before revealing the grander means by which each story is connected, tying each to the other, you to them, and thereby us to one another.

Conners has once again charged me with composing the Outroduction.

And, so, I shall endeavor, this time, instead of launching a vain and sportive attempt to link that which you have just read (or, will soon read, should you, dear reader, be among the class of rebel-natured literature consumers who enjoy scanning the final chapter of a book before starting it)—this time I shall strive to cast a ray of light upon the yet rather obscured visage that is Conners, doing so now in a more sincere manner. Although I cannot say for sure that I will not, at some point in the writing of this Outroduction, end up linking these seven tales in some manner or other, or hurling a quick jab at the proverbial (or, perhaps, literal) ribs of my employer, what follows will nonetheless be a free-flowing reflection, presented for the very same reason these books of Ramblings have been compiled.

There is no work the Author loves better than storytelling. It is no pastime for him, no hobby; it is his joyful labor, the work that inspires and enlivens him; putting pen to page, or finger to keys (yes, a non-plural *finger*—did you know Conners can type with only his index fingers, a method he calls "seek and destroy typing?")—the composing and pursuing the fruition of a story is my employer's deep passion, a never-ending source of joy; it is something so precious to him that I know he will continue to etch away his cherished tales, even if not one person on this earth ever cares to give his work a read.

You, dear reader, are a major reason why Conners writes—he so earnestly wants to create something you will enjoy, something that will inspire you, make you take a second thought, or simply fill your soul with the soothing medicine of laughter. He wants his work to touch you; but, should these words be penned only for the page that lies atop them within the closed book, know that Conners would lose not a drop of the immense, almost inexplicable, overabundant elation he experiences whilst composing, nor suffer any loss of the satisfaction that comes from pouring out as an ocean of water over the edge of a towering cliff one of the many tales pressing desperately upon his heart, yearning for release.

For my employer, writing is a gift. He claims not to be among even those whose writing is called good, much less hold a seat amidst the greats of the literary world; for such would be an untrue assertion. Rather, it is the joy of writing—the process itself: of scrawling, of inventing, of storytelling—that he knows for sure is something that has been given freely to a most undeserving recipient. His hands were imbued with the means to experience this great joy of writing; thus, he feels charged with a great responsibility.

"Who am I to have been granted stewardship of something as mighty and wonderful as this?" I once heard him say. "And what with it am I to do?"

He will not change the world. Whatever skill he might possess (I'll leave that to you to analyze and decide) is of less than little consequence in the daily struggle that is life, against which his own troubles, and mine, mean nothing—in what little we may think we possess, are we not kings among the world of men?

This gift from which he draws selfish delight is worthless in his hands. And he is no one to be revered or remembered. But if through this benison and source of undeserved joy a part of that blessing might be passed on to another, if his words can somehow be used for something greater than what can be found in his own enjoyment in etching them, perhaps then he will know, in part, the answer to his question.

Things are changing, my dear reader. Indeed, things have changed. And what lies in the offing is uncertain. But it is not without hope.

How, though, could this be true, you might wonder? For did not Conners himself demonstrate in the leading lineup of this collection a series of this world's most devastating reflections?

And, from these, what was offered in the end?

To what light were you, dear reader, directed when fell the final stroke of the pen?

There can be no more valid point than that.

While Conners has ever been skeptical of the position that artistic output finds its genesis in the creator's present state of mind or being, he would never deny the influence or inspiration found therein. I wonder, though, if he's since modified his stance—not to say that there can be no other genesis than the latter suggested, but rather to better acknowledge the true potency said factors have upon a piece. One who is filled with sadness can wield words of happiness, but can not the reader identify the hollowness of those words? If, say, Conners were to employ his skill in an effort to fabricate light, when in him is darkness, has he naught but deceived, cast a clever veil over the eyes of the casual peruser and dazzled their eyes, mind, and spirit with sparks like fireworks that burst in bright colors and deafening sounds, only to quickly pass away and leave a layer of cloud to paint an already blackened night? See here in these tales that which was true in Conners when they were composed: hopelessness; and see here in the final tale—begun long before the rest and penned over the course of several years; its intended message and ending amended—a depth of darkness and hopelessness to which none of the latter had sunk; yet, in its end…well, things changed.

What, now, can I tell you?

Indeed, the section preceding the last in this Outroduction had been all I had intended to pen—this and the latter section are two new additions in what is my second go at composing a closing, one that has effectively doubled its length.

It seems this theme has a mind of its own.

What can I say of Conners?

What can I say of that which is to come?

Of all the diverse criticism and feedback he has received

over the course of his career, there has been one constant—to this have I already alluded: that his are pieces beset with great darkness and shrouded, as we've discussed, with hopelessness. And this criticism, though never dismissed, he has chosen to let lie still, to neither touch nor of it speak; for of what else could the vessel Conners compose?

Things have changed.

This collection is a reflection of that: a revelation of its progression (*On the Wall*, as you might have guessed, while it can be fitted into the overall puzzle, was selected more so as a diversionary piece to ease what Conners feared had become a dark and downbound train, whence readers were likely to begin bailing if not given a little levity, and quickly).

My employer…well, I don't know what he is. Nor could I tell you where he is. (Given the occupancy of the cookie jar being that of crumbs and air, I'd be pretty confident if I had to guess where he's been). But, of course, I mean not location. I've seen the way he watches the world; I've felt the weight of his wonder; I know the depth of his grief. In these, he is unchanged; such you will see in many of his works already penned when at last they are released. But not one work in progress, nor any in the offing, will carry the same burden as those that came before, the last of which rest here.

I cannot imagine it will be so.

What can I claim he has attained?

No more than he would claim.

Perhaps, that is naught but faith, hope…even love.

Seeking it was a conscious decision.

Attaining it was Christ.

And, so, like one of whom you may read in a forthcoming

novel, he who eomplys this hand continues to pour over the map, trusting only that the way is true.

I can but observe and wonder where the next step might fall.

Farewell,

Your Faithful Narrator

THE END

SNEAK PEEK AT A NEW NOVEL BY C. K. CONNERS

Preview Prologue: Adam & Adeline

LANGUAGEis a funny thing. (Yes, I'm doing another deep dive into words). Recently, I was feeling rather, shall we say, not myself. In times such as these, one is, I believe, at one's most vulnerable; for if one's feelings suddenly go astray, disentangling themselves from the very soul to which they have been divinely matched, one is liable to experience some rather less-than-desirable things.

First, one will undoubtedly experience confusion. If one is not oneself, who is one? It is very literally an out-of-body experience—and whose body is it? The next door neighbor's? Someone from history, or perhaps a sort of future roamer of vast and distant cosmic spaces? Maybe the squirrel in a nearby tree?

As I pondered this, I realized something funny about myself; perhaps, dear reader, you will be able to relate: While it seemed nearly impossible to find any sort of sense, reason, or comfort in the "self" of a living (or, formerly living) person or creature, I could easily relate with the feelings of inanimate objects. I found I am an expert in the feelings of doormats, old gloves, rogue balloons—all sorts of things! If ever I found myself not myself, but rather the self of a doormat, I'd wholly appreciate the sensation of having dirty, muddy shoes pressed against and wiped across my face; or, if ever I felt like a rogue balloon, I'd know intimately the thrill of flight and wide open, unbounded freedom, heading straight and true for an Icarian doom.

This day, however, I wasn't feeling like any rodents or common household objects; I was feeling rather ill—physically speaking. Amid an intense ponderation of my situation, I sought some words to best describe my present state (like counting sheep, we literary professionals count our adjectives, nouns, conjunctions, etcetera to set ourselves into a lulled state). And as I was reciting my mental thesaurus, the word "miserable" came to mind.

True, indeed, as is used the word, I felt miserable. However, my state of "*ehh*-ness" had rendered my brain just numb enough to idly turn about in its mental fingers this trisyllabic (or, for the more distinguished speakers, quadrisyllabic) adjective.

Miserable.

Miser—able.

Misery able.

Able to experience misery.

How interesting, thought I: a combination of two words, a contraction, creating both a new word and a message (***Post Composition Note:*** *Seems the illness was still affecting my brain when this was first composed; for is not that revelation the basic function of language?*). Not unlike the conceiving of a child, elements from both contributors help design the newborn; thus, we can state with confidence that while something new is created, something existing, used to forge that new thing, holds yet its distinction—in this case, its meaning. We can, therefore, conclude that we must ALWAYS be miserable, for we ever hold the capacity to experience misery!

And, so, I became depressed.

Can this be true?

Must I be forever miserable?

Perhaps, thought I, there is a word to counter it! A word, like "happy"—an antithesis to "miserable."

Joyful.

No.

That means to be full of joy. It's a state I can achieve, but, unfortunately, not something for which I inherently have the capacity.

Such would be "joyable."

Cheerful.

Darn it! Again with the being-full-of words!

Gleeful.

Mirthful.

Blissful

NO MORE "-FUL" WORDS!

But that was just it! Many of the words under the umbrella of "happy" celebrated the state of being filled with said wonderful prefix! Sure, there were more synonyms, like jubilant and euphoric; but I'd become too lost in this trail of thought to even consider them—is not the modern scientific method to disregard evidences in contrast with one's *trutheory*?

I then considered "comfortable."

Yes! Comfortable! Able to experience comfort!

How marvelous!

Comfort can make one happy, right?

Sure it can!

Then, I remembered the unfortunate existence of the word "*un*comfortable."

Rats.

Since I have the capacity to both experience and not experience comfort, it seemed this once promising trail had ended in a wash. Furthermore, this wash suggested that, if indeed these words canceled each other out, there exists no capacity whatsoever to either experience or not experience comfort! If I am able to encounter both, can I encounter either? No, it seems!

I can't say I'm terribly comfortable with that.

Then, the word "awful" came to mind.

Though my train of thought had already derailed into incredible territory—incredible, in that I was blowing my ailing mind with poorly prepared theories lacking *any* credibility—I rocketed to my feet with a triumphant, "A-HA!" Some ten minutes later, I regained consciousness; though, my skull still pounded from the sudden head rush that had led to black walls closing in over my eyes before the floor left my feet and gave the one side of my face a good ol' slap. Once I'd successfully recalled my own name and assured myself that the owner of the floor on which I'd drooled would be understanding, I pondered the depths of the word "awful."

Used mainly to describe things so filled with dreadful horrors that they radiate sensory stimulants of a most foul nature, and other times used to punctuate a tremendous amount of something, I began to wonder if we've been using the word incorrectly all along.

Another contraction, the words "awe" and "full" seem first to have been joined to describe something that fills one with wonderment or dread—thus, our present employment of the word demonstrates a logical progression from this point. However, the longer I basked in my indisposed state, the more I became convinced that my theory of misuse might just be true.

A contraction, as I have stated; but not the one described in the dictionaries. Instead of "awe" being the leading half of our word, we can suppose that, rather than having dropped an "e" from the first word to form the new one, a "w" has instead been dropped, making our leading word "aww;" therefore, I propose that "awful" was, in point of theory, intended originally to convey the exact opposite of what it speaks today.

To demonstrate:

"Hi, Mabel!"

"Why, hello, John!"

"How are you on this fine, *fantastitabulous* day?"

"Awful!"

"Dear me! What is it that has left you in such a sensational state of being?"

"Only this: that I have been irreparably infected!"

"Goodness! By what, pray tell? By what? And might this infection be so severe as to be contagious?"

"I will tell all of this most contagious infection! Today, good sir, I attended a puppy pampering convention, and I have been spilling *aww*s from my lips ever since! I am simply filled with awws!"

"Awful, indeed!"

Need you more proof?

It seems our understanding of the language we speak—so well now that it has become our nature to do so—is not quite as sound as we might have thought. Sure, this analysis is the product of a brain seeped in the soup of ailing flesh and over-the-counter drugs; but is there no truth at all to be found herein? Are we not "awful" when so moved by cuteness that we cannot help but speak an abundance of awws? And are we, who hold the capacity for misery, not always miserable?

If I might exercise a bit of insanity for a moment by offering thee a scrap of thanks: forsooth, I know now my capacity to experience misery, after having sat through this entire rambling mess of—

Pardon me, my dear, eloquent reader; but I must direct your attention to this book's title.

I submitted to this text to peruse the ramblings of ONE: those of the Author, and not his insufferable lackey!

A lackey, am I? Thou dost wound me, dear reader! For I am a professional, hired to do a job; and if the rambler himself has found this waggish tongue of mine unfit to be conveyed through my fingers and onto the page, then he would not have contracted me for this sequel, as well as his most grand and elaborate piece, yet to come. I suggest you take five and grab a tall glass of milk and plate of cookies.

Thou wouldst dare presume that I have no dietary restrictions, and, thus, could digest sugary, gluten-laden, dairy delights? Wouldst thou even tempt one teetering on the tightrope of body mass maintenance? Hast thou no concern for my wellbeing?

I love you, dear reader; I mean that—therefore, I will tell you that I believe you expel far too much energy on one who seems to bother you to your fiery core.

Depart! Find your respite and desired delight! But return posthaste, and attend to this: the final "ramble."

They say misery loves company, and in this next story, two players will test their own limits of wretchedness and woe.

Adam & Adeline was first conceived in 2015 as a tale bending toward the lighthearted mockery of magical storylines, drawing inspiration from old fairy tales to do so. However, after the first few pages had been composed, the Author suddenly found himself rather dissatisfied with the story's direction; and, immediately thereafter, the tale was shelved.

For years it sat in a pile of doomed pieces: a lone computer folder housing misfit narratives the Author has lost the inspiration and/or interest to complete. Yet, *Adam & Adeline* was far from forgotten; for the Author did so enjoy that which had for this piece first been written on that cool, September midnight; he just could see no purpose in bringing the original inspiration into full realization.

And then it happened.

The year was 2018. Ramblings One had just been published. Ramblings Two was in the works. And, looking to add another story to the mix, Conners' gaze returned to *Adam & Adeline.*

I very much enjoy telling this part of the story, dear reader, for it involves the rare occurrence of my work being commended by my employer. Pleasantries, encouragements, and even salutations, are rarely exchanged in the one-room office of Route 27 Publishing®. Usually, one must infer the finer sentiments from the other; the harsher sentiments flow freely.

As I have said, I love this part of the story; because, you see, that which had been originally composed had been so done by yours truly!

Thou?

I, indeed!

While every single Ramblings Series story up to this very moment has been penned solely by the Author, this piece, my dear reader, marks the first of my own brushstrokes as Conners' official narrator. And when he fished back through his work-on-pause and read once again the words that had earned me this job, he had no choice but to actually—with words…falling from his mouth hole—say, "Well done, you rascally rapscallion. Now, let's get to work."

Of course, I just had to (and did) point out that his chosen adjective for describing me made the modification of the following noun a redundancy—a point which made the moment all the more glorious!

"You might as well have called me an idiotic idiot!"

In his defense (if I'm loony enough to offer him one), the composition of his insult is not exactly uncommon. Either way, I got my gold star—he *had* to give it to me!

All elation aside, he sat me down and told me that, while he wanted to keep some of the same lighthearted spirit that I had inserted into the original pages, he had been pondering a DRASTICALLY different approach, purpose, and ultimate destination, one leading not to Ramblings Two, but rather to a title all its own.

This we discussed.

And, I must say, dear reader, I was surprised.

A direction such as the one he proposed was explicitly outside the arena in which he normally operated.

Even now, and with no diminishment to its original effect, I am amazed by what he said to me that day. Those words, however, I cannot share here. They are, instead, printed upon the pages soon to be released.

How can someone be made to want something that is one hundred percent, without a doubt, no question, hands down a fantasy?

Author Bio

C. K. Conners was born sometime, somewhere, and is still alive elsewhere. He is known by some as a hopeless romantic, a wearying wit, a formidably fluent fantasist, but most of all, *Who?*

When he's not writing about himself in the third person, this *what's-his-name* can be found flying in his private jet to exotic places, wine tasting with international business moguls, or philosophizing in robes and sandals on the steps of academia with fellow, curious-minded pupils—or, to put it more accurately, one can usually assume with confidence that on any given day Conners is locked in his room, wearing holey sweatpants and tattered moccasins, rocking a bedhead hairdo that would make Einstein jealous, sitting hunched over a blank piece of paper, and carving thereon the chicken scratch hieroglyphs he hopes to one day pass off as novels.

If he were, in any way, an interesting person, perhaps more than this could be relayed. But, alas, he is about as common as a scraped knee, and equally agreeable.

Route 27 Publishing

Founded in April 2018 by author C. K. Conners, Route 27 Publishing® and its children's books imprint Randy Boy Books® feature exclusively the literary madness produced by its founder, CEO, and bearer of basically every other company role. Though presently comparable in earnings to a not-for-profit organization, Route 27 Publishing® aims to one day grow large enough to employ full-time its founder, CEO, etcetera, etcetera, and bring into the public light all the tales he so desires to tell before his journey comes to an end.

Other Connerian Titles

Adam & Adeline

The Ramblings of a Small-Town What's-His-Name

Table 9

www.ingramcontent.com/pod-product-compliance
Lightning Source LLC
LaVergne TN
LVHW091137080826
845145LV00008B/2176

* 9 7 8 1 9 4 9 0 4 5 0 2 4 *